Carpe Diem

A time of pleasure

Another erotic story

By

"J" Erotica

Carpe Diem is a work of fiction and all characters and places are the creation of the author's imagination. The work is copyrighted by LWPublications 2011

ISBN-13:

978-0615545141 (LWPublications, Inc)

ISBN-10:

0615545149

© LWPublications

7 Dey Street

Suite 207

New York, NY 10007

Dedicated to those who love
and are willing to be free.

Chapter 1

The computer screen taunted Sandy, as she felt the pangs of desire move through her body, settling mainly between her legs. It was warm in her apartment, yet she knew the perspiration between her breasts wasn't from the furnace; at least not the one in the basement of her building.

Sitting in the hollow light of the Internet video as it flooded her space, she watched the sexual equipment on the well-hung male become larger before her eyes. The cause of this transformation was mainly from the concerted effort of a big-breasted blonde female kneeling and sucking on his manhood. Sandy felt her pulse quicken as his now gleaming wet steel rod appeared on her screen. Rubbing the perspiration from her forehead, she watched as her Stud Man took the blonde and threw her on the bed. Sandy's breathing became shorter as Stud Man aggressively pulled the blonde's legs apart and stood over her naked body stroking his huge dick.

"That thing is enormous," Sandy muttered, quickly looking around to be sure nobody heard her. It was a stupid move; her only sex partner tonight was the flashing computer screen, mocking her empty life with putrid fantasy. Feeling a sense of futility, she reached to turn off the screen just as Stud Man began to push his enormous rod into the blonde's glistening pussy. Hesitating, Sandy waited to see if he could actually get it inside the small opening presented by the blonde. The camera moved closer to the action, while Sandy's hands moved from her laptop to her lap. Spreading her legs, she began to touch the flimsy material confining her now screaming pussy.

The camera closed in on his steel-hard dick as it began to penetrate the female's folds of skin. Pulling out, his dick now glistened with the wetness of the blonde's deepest recesses. Stud Man spread her lips further apart and then pushed in deeper and deeper.

Sandy felt the cloth under her fingers become moist as she rubbed a little harder. Sliding it aside, she spread her own wet lips, slowly beginning to run her fingers up and down the slick, hot space demanding her attention. The blonde pulled her legs further back, as Stud Man penetrated her with the full extension of his massive erection, forcing Sandy to push into her own beckoning vagina.

Unable to reach deep, she stood, pulled off her underpants, sat down in the chair and spread her legs on each side of the computer screen. The flashing strobes of light flickering on her now naked garden of pleasure provided a guide as her fingers danced over the sensitive places, sending electricity through her body. Using her free hand, she pulled her T-shirt over her head, threw it off and began to message her breast as she pushed deeper into her throbbing vagina.

Stud Man now turned the blonde over, positioning her ass in the air. Spreading her cheeks, he rubbed his huge dick on her quivering vagina, and then shoved into her violently. Increasing his tempo, the blonde's tits began to sway with the impact of his fucking as Sandy pushed into her own playground. Feeling her fingers getting wetter, she dove deeper trying to maintain the same rhythm as Stud Man. Releasing her breast, she moved her free hand to her clit and exposed it to her touch, discovering it was very hard and very needy.

Stud Man continued to slam away at the blonde who was definitely in the throws of orgasmic delight. Sandy pulled her legs back as she frantically rubbed

7

her pulsating clit. She felt pressure inside her build until she sensed splattering on her legs and ass. Her garden of pleasure was about to become a river of orgasm soaking her body and floor; she chose to ignore the outpouring of her passion.

Stud Man was sweating and banging harder as Sandy felt the growing pangs of orgasm build in her groin. "Hurry up," she groaned, trying to hang on to her climax until Stud Man did the same. At last, he pulled out, turned the blonde over, and rapidly stroked his erection over her bulging tits. Sandy grabbed her pussy, jammed her fingers deep inside, frantically rubbing her clit until at last she and Stud Man both ejaculated into the world around them. While his load fell on the naked breasts of the blonde, Sandy's ran down her ass like a river finally falling into a large puddle below her chair. Leaning back she slowly brought her feet to the floor, trying to avoid the wetness below. It didn't happen often, but when she was overly horny, she became a waterfall that would soak everything around her.

Walking to the kitchen, Sandy glanced at her naked reflection in the mirror. Things had improved over the last two years. She no longer cringed at the woman in the mirror who'd somehow grown into a rapidly aging, overweight, divorce-ravaged victim. She'd vowed to recover her lost self and two years of therapy, dieting, gym workouts, and freedom from the piece of shit known as her ex-husband had contributed to the woman she now viewed before her.

At forty-two she'd regained her waistline coupled with trim hips, nicely rounded ass, and well-proportioned natural breasts. She wished her tummy was muscular but settled with the fact that it was soft yet flat; an okay exception at her age. Her dark hair was a return to her pre-blonde days, and she liked how it framed her green eyes. Thinking about the blonde in the video, she was happy she'd returned to her natural dark color.

Turning from the mirror, she journeyed into the kitchen, picked up the role of paper towels, and then headed back to clean up her vaginal-river remains. Throwing the towel pieces on the floor, Sandy once again looked at her computer screen, observing the other twenty-four videos offered; all of which provided a stimulus for those who needed to masturbate through their sexually empty lives.

Closing the laptop, she picked up her wet underwear along with her hastily discarded shirt and, with a deep sigh, headed to her bed. As usual with her Internet sex parties, she felt even emptier at the end than she had at the beginning. For the millionth time Sandy vowed she had to do something about her empty sex life. Turning out the light, she drifted into a discontented sleep.

10

Chapter 2

Justin Armond Betterly Jr. hated
mornings. In fact, Justin Armond Betterly
Jr. hated most things in his life but
couldn't figure out how to make changes.
The reason for this was Justin Armond
Betterly Sr., his powerful asshole
father, who had demanded that Justin Jr.
live a life reflecting the status of the
Betterly name and fortune.

"Be a fucking man and stop
whimpering," was the boot-camp training
his father gave him as a child; never
taking into consideration that the
whimpering child missed his dead mother.

"You will not draw negative
attention to yourself at any time or I
will beat you until you can't walk." Such
a compassionate man was his fucked-up
father.

When Justin was old enough to make
decisions on his own, he did everything
he could to piss off his father. This was
an ongoing campaign until his father died
in an airplane crash outside of Paris.
Within days, Justin Jr., a thirty-five-
year-old playboy millionaire, was
suddenly CEO of Betterly Enterprise
International, subject to the scrutiny of
a board of directors who didn't trust him
and four thousand employees who assumed
he would take care of them. For the last
ten years, he'd followed the well-worn
pathway of his deceased father, leading
the company in a discipline that
amazingly caused it to flourish under his
direction.

He'd hated every day of the last ten
years. He'd especially hated the last
year as he negotiated with a takeover
company who finally bought out his shares
for a tidy sum of over nine hundred fifty
million dollars. After the fucking
lawyers, tax collectors, accountants and

other assholes got through, he was left with slightly over seven hundred fifty million and an empty life. And Justin still truly hated every day.

Throwing back the covers, he headed to the bathroom to try to wash away some of the shit his life had become. He knew it wouldn't work any more than the thousand other things he tried in order to feel better about living. In the end, nothing really brought him any sense of pleasure or purpose. His father repeatedly told him he was a worthless shit and no matter how successfully Justin had finally run the old man's company he could never get his dead father's words out of his mind.

Exiting the shower, he wandered back to his bed, empty as usual. He'd filled it with two wives and a bundle of women, but it always ended up empty. The wives and the bundle of women all wanted a part of Justin Armond Betterly Jr.: The part that began with a dollar sign and ended

with a dollar sign. In the end, they all
got fucked and so did he. They just
seemed to prosper in it better than he
did.

Looking around the room, Justin
Armond Betterly Jr. came to a decision
that actually brought a smile to his
face. He was forty-five, educated,
wealthy, in good health, and unattached
to anyone or anything. Pulling on a pair
of jeans and a sweatshirt, Justin went to
his desk, opened the drawer, took out a
checkbook and a thousand dollars in cash
he kept for change. Looking around the
room, he smiled again and exited.

Justin Armond Betterly Jr. had made
a decision. He was going to disappear,
and all the people who might think it was
a bad idea could go fuck themselves.

Chapter 3

Jammed together in a subway car so filthy it defied explanation, Sandy rode to Chambers Street heading to Starbucks for her morning wakeup. The day was overcast and dull, although the chill of winter was not as prevalent as it had been since December. She loved New York but hated winter.

Picking up her double latte at a price that could feed a poor family in some countries, she headed toward her office on Fulton Street. The construction continued on the World Trade Center, but it always looked like a lot of activity with no progress. She'd been out of town when the Towers fell yet felt the impact deeply in her very soul. Ten years later, it was still hard to grasp the enormity of destruction that horrible day caused in so many lives.

Entering the lobby of her building, she smiled as Andrew looked up and waved at her. "Mornin', Ms. Carlyle. How you doin' this fine day?"

Andrew's greeting was the same every morning for the last five years. Rumor had it he'd been in the building since it was constructed fifty-three years ago, which may have been true, but Sandy doubted it. Andrew was a kind and loving person who brought a little joy to her life each morning.

"Good morning, Andrew. How are you feeling today?"

"Doin' okay for an old man, Ms. Carlyle, but even if I wasn't, wouldn't do no good to complain. You got an envelope here that was delivered late last night I guess. It was here when I got in taday."

Sandy thanked him, took the envelope and headed to the elevator. She glanced at the return address, which indicated Allen Tours and was marked special delivery. Reaching her floor, she stuffed the envelope in the side of her briefcase and headed to her office. The door was unlocked indicating Gladys was already there. The two of them had never set any fixed hours since they started working together, yet they always seemed to balance out obligations without any fixed schedule.

Sandy had been an editor with a large publisher for nine years until she decided to go freelance about ten years ago. She'd known Gladys from several joint projects they'd worked on, and when Sandy told her she was going independent Gladys wanted to know if she wanted some company. The two of them worked well together and prospered enough over the last ten years to keep both of them comfortable even if not rich. Gladys was in her mid-fifty's and married with two older children. Sandy was part of Gladys' family and loved her kids like they were her own.

Sandy wanted children at one point in her life, but after eight years of marriage to Erick, she decided neither marriage nor parenting were really part of her journey. She and Erick met at a business conference, dated for about a year and then for some insane reason, decided to get married. On her honeymoon, she caught him screwing some bimbo in the parking lot, and it had gone downhill from there. Erick was a shit who couldn't keep his dick in his pants or a dollar in his pocket. When they divorced he was up to his neck in personal debt that she didn't have any part of and had some woman in Boston claiming he was the father of her child. Sandy crawled away from the marriage a broken, angry, empty mess. She'd made a comeback, but the scars of that season went deep in her heart.

"That you Sandy?" Gladys called out from her office.

"Tis me. You're in early today. What's happening?"

Sandy entered Gladys's office, which always reminded her of a room hit by a tornado. Gladys was officially the most disorganized person Sandy had ever known, but the work she produced was exact and the most professional available. Sandy wasn't sure how Gladys did it, but somehow it worked.

"I've got that last draft on the Wall Street book that has to go out this week, so I decided to hit it early before I got distracted. You look tired. Are you okay?"

Gladys was like a mother hen to Sandy, acting as her protector and life coach since the divorce. Gladys was a bit on the chubby side and with her greyish-brown hair, she seemed very much the maternal type.

"I was restless last night and didn't get to sleep until late," Sandy replied. What she didn't say was how her little computer sex event lasted until three in the morning, allowing only four hours of sleep.

"You need to take a break, honey," Gladys said as she returned to her work, "this has been a long winter."

Walking across the hall to her office, Sandy remembered the envelope Andrew gave her. Setting down her purse and briefcase, she opened it, finding a letter and a brochure enclosed. Opening the letter, she read:

Dear Ms. Carlyle

Mr. John Rawlings recommended I contact you, as you have been a great service to his company. My family owns a charter operation out of Palm Beach Florida, and we have put together a book about life on a charter boat, which we are hoping to distribute to our customers and to other boating enthusiasts. We have contracted with a printer but have decided to self-publish rather that get involved with a publishing company. The book needs professional editing, which is why I am contacting you. I would like to hire your services as an editor but with one unusual request. I would like you to do the editing work on one of our charters here in Palm Beach. The adventure of a charter cruise is an unusual experience, and we want the book to reflect that feeling. The other problem is time. We need to begin the final editing and evaluation in two weeks.

I recognize this is an unusual request, but I do hope you can assist us. I look forward to your reply. You may call me or email me at the address above. For your information, I am enclosing a brochure about our charters.

I look forward to hearing from you.

Sincerely yours,

Fredrich Allen

President, Allen Tours. Inc.

Sandy opened the brochure showing beautiful sailboats and cabin cruisers in lush tropical waters. Allen Tours apparently sailed out of Palm Beach providing seven-day or longer cruises to the islands and into the Keys. There were no prices, but the brochure proclaimed without words that these were charters for those who had money. She reread the letter and then leaned back looking out her window. Seven days paid work in the tropics or seven days paid work in windy, cold, snowy Manhattan. Fredrich Allen hadn't mentioned anything about fees, but she knew John Rawlings well, and if he recommended her to Fredrich, then she was sure John indicated she wasn't cheap. She and Gladys had done several jobs for John over the years and always charged top dollar. John appreciated the thoroughness of their work: never questioning the cost.

She and Gladys weren't greedy businesswomen, but they did value personal time and knew the quality of their work was well respected in the industry. Most of their clients were corporate accounts who became repeat customers over the years. She glanced at the letter again, opened her laptop to her Safari Internet, located her email account, and drafted a reply.

Mr. Allen — Thank you for your letter and offer. While the time constraints are somewhat difficult, the potential of being out of New York in the winter is of considerable value. I appreciate John Rawlings referral, and I trust he provided some of our work for your review. I will be happy to come to Florida in a week to begin the process you require. I am attaching our fee schedule and sample contract, which you can update to reflect your needs. Let me know if this meets with your approval. Sandy Carlyle

She sent another quick note to John Rawlings thanking him for the referral and then plunged into her daily work. The break would be great but for now reality called.

Chapter 4

After two hours of fighting traffic on route 95, Justin decided to pull into the nearest restaurant parking lot just to get out of the car. Thus far, his escape had been a disaster as the first few days proved Miami was simply not his kind of town. He'd never visited before but was intrigued with some of the pictures he'd seen in travel magazines. He flew into Miami International and spent three days exploring the city. While interesting and beautiful, it was just not his cup of tea. The women were hot and the clubs were active party spots. Nevertheless, it was just too vigorous for his needs.

The restaurant he entered was just off highway 95 and appeared to be a relic left over from the 50's. The lobby had an empty bar on the left, which looked inviting but not at the current hour. Along the wall was a lighted cabinet displaying several plates of desserts, which had the appearance of having overstayed their expiration date. While he waited for the hostess, Justin noticed a rack of flyers describing different activities in the local area. He grabbed a few along with the local paper and then followed the hostess to a booth in the rear.

After ordering, he opened the paper, which indicated he was in Palm Beach. When leaving Miami he'd decided to just drive until he was tired of driving. In spite of his decision to disappear, he was having trouble figuring out what to do or where to go. Before his father died, his guideline had been to go wherever and do whatever pissed his father off the most. During the last ten years, the pressures and politics of

running a large corporation guided him.
Now there was nothing to provide
direction. He decided to go to Florida
because he was sick of cold and wanted to
see some color other than grey. That
decision propelled him to this second-
class diner outside of Palm Beach without
a clue of what to do next. Something had
to change if this new direction in his
life was to work.

He scanned the paper but found
nothing of interest, so he pulled up the
flyers he'd gathered on the way into the
diner. Two were brochures trying to sell
fishing expeditions in the offshore
water. He'd done enough of those to know
he didn't need someone to drive him
around and bait his hook. He'd fished the
Mediterranean and the Australian coast,
which would be a lot more difficult than
the Atlantic waters around Palm Beach.
Another flyer talked about some museum he
had no interest in seeing.

The last one was for a tour company
providing private cruises through the
islands of the southern Atlantic down to
the lower Keys. They showed a beautiful
sixty-foot Cal with full sails on her
twin mast sailing in clear blue water.
He'd sailed on a seventy-foot Cal when he
was twenty-five and loved the experience.
However, what caught his eye was the
Couach 125 yacht on the next page. He
owned a Couach 71, which was currently
docked in southern California. He hadn't
been on it in over a year because of the
buyout crap but kept a crew on the boat
full time. The Couach 125 was a dreamboat
he'd never seen before, but he knew from
experience it was not only a luxury yacht
but also a damn fine handling ship.

    He was interrupted by the arrival of
his order but kept thinking about the 125
as he dug into his burger. That would be
a great way to disappear. Hell, for a
million bucks he could probably rent it
out for a year and just keep moving

around. Chewing on his burger he thought about the idea, then decided it would draw way too much attention, something he wanted to avoid. No, he couldn't just drop his money on people and keep a low profile; nevertheless, he sure could take some time to go look at the yacht.

Finishing his lunch, he checked the address for the tour company and punched it into the GPS in his phone, which located the dock and charted out a map to follow. For the first time in months, Justin actually felt excited about something, and with a smile, he left the parking lot heading into Palm Beach Harbor.

About a half hour later, he located a sign pointing to Allen Tours, the company that produced the brochure. Pulling into the Marina, he quickly spotted the Couach 125 sitting at the far end of the dock. Her white hull gleamed in the midday sun making her look like a huge glacier floating on blue water. The aft deck stood high above the dock with railings of magnificently polished teak wood. Looking up to the main deck, he could see the bridge antennas indicating it was equipped with all the latest navigation aids, but the ship was too high to make out any further details.

Parking his car, he proceeded down the dock to get a closer look but was disappointed to find a locked gate blocking the passage.

"Can I help you?" a voice called out from behind him. Turning, he saw a man in shorts and a crew shirt walking toward him.

"Just admiring the Couach 125," Justin said, as the man approached. "She's a magnificent ship."

"That she is," said the approaching stranger extending his hand, "but she is an expensive little whore who can have a real bad temper. I'm Fredrich Allen, the sometimes-happy owner of the *Eclipse*."

Justin grasped the extended hand.
"Justin," he said, deciding not to give
out too much information.

"I was just going to pick up
something in the main cabin," Fredrich
indicated as he unlocked the gate. "Want
to take a look at her for a minute?"

"Thanks a lot. That would be a real
treat. I crewed on a Couach 71' but never
was on the 125 foot," Justin said. "I
know what you mean about bad temper; push
her the wrong way, and she will make you
pay. The 71 ' had twin 1300 hp; what does
this have?"

"This sweetheart holds twin 2000
horse power and has a top speed of 28
knots," Fredrich said as he opened the
transom gate and stepped aboard. Justin
followed, admiring the beauty of the aft
deck, a polished wood complete with bar
and a lounge that simply said 'class.'

Fredrich unlocked the rear door and
stepped back for Justin to enter. "She
sleeps eight guests and four crew. She

was launched in 2009, and we picked her up two years ago."

Justin was no stranger to luxury and quickly discerned that the Couach 125' was a well-built and well-trimmed yacht. He followed Fredrich up to the bridge where he was confronted with the finest electronics money could buy. Every radar, sonar, GPS, radio, and other state-of-the-art navigation tools proclaimed this was a first class ship.

"This is magnificent, Fredrich. I'm truly impressed with the caliber of electronics and navigation."

Fredrich smiled. "You ever run a ship like this?"

Justin hesitated and then replied, "I have a fifty-ton captain's license and maritime clearance for one this size, but the 71 foot is the biggest I've handled."

Fredrich turned to look at Justin. "So you didn't just crew the 71 foot, you captained it?"

"Sort of. It's a little complicated, but I ran her most of the time." Justin again didn't want to give too much information about owning the 71 foot.

"If you don't mind my asking, what brings you to the dock? You live in Palm Beach?"

Justin, feeling a little uncomfortable with the direct questions, replied, "Just passing through. I'm looking to escape for a while and tried Miami. It was okay but not for very long. I stopped for lunch up on 95 and saw your flyer. I wanted to see the 125 foot up close."

"That's really weird," Fredrich replied. "Not your trip from Miami, but the fact you just showed up here. I have an excursion today and my assistant is out sick. I came down here to get a list of people who'd be able to help skipper the ship with me, and then you show up. You have a fifty-ton license and know how

to run a 71 foot. That is weird. You
lookin' for work?"

Justin was a little taken back at
the offer. In reality, he wasn't looking
to do anything, but the thought of being
on the *Eclipse* was a powerful draw. "Not
looking for anything long-term but would
be glad to help out short-term."

Fredrich smiled. "That's perfect. I
have a special cruise with just one
passenger who's working on a project for
me. She flies in tonight, and we'll leave
the dock when she is settled. We won't be
out more than two days and three nights.
I'll handle most of the work on the ship;
you just have to keep us on course and
run the bridge. You have your maritime
information handy so I can book you in
properly?"

Justin hesitated for a second.
Giving the information would be a full
disclosure of who he was and that didn't
fit into his plans. Fredrich probably
wouldn't know him, but any smart captain

would do a search before he left the dock with a new hand. "I have the documents in my luggage, but I have a little problem. I'm trying to remain anonymous for personal reasons, and I'm sure you'll know more about me before we leave, so my only request is you keep whatever you find private between you and me."

Fredrich looked at him and asked, "You running from the law?"

Justin laughed, "No, not even from a parking ticket. I'm just trying to keep a low profile for personal reasons. You'll probably know more after you do a record search. If we can keep what you find between us, I'll take the trip without pay. It would be enough pay just to run the *Eclipse*."

Fredrich stuck out his hand. "You got a deal as long as you're not bringing trouble with you."

Justin grasped the outstretched hand. "That, I guarantee, is not a problem. I look forward to serving on your ship, Captain."

Fredrich laughed. "Hell, for free I might try to keep you on forever."

Chapter 5

Sandy closed her laptop, as the flight attendant announced they were preparing to land at Palm Beach International Airport where the weather was clear and eighty degrees. Having received the email book draft from Fredrich, she read through the pages on the trip from New York in order to get a better idea of what the project required. The story lines needed some cleanup and restructuring, but it was well written and informative. The book was a narrative about life on the charter boats and the different incidents guests experienced over the years. Allen Tours obviously catered to the very wealthy, and she assumed the tour company received permission to use the stories and names mentioned in the book. Fredrich indicated in his note the final copy would have a lot of pictures, but they were not attached to the manuscript.

Sandy closed her eyes as the landing gear deployed and the plane contacted the ground. She wondered what it would be like to have so much money you could travel all over the world and not have to have concerns about anything. Well, at least she was going to have a few days to soak up the atmosphere and feel like the rich and privileged. Even if it was work oriented, this was still a welcomed break from her life in Manhattan.

After taxiing to the gate, Sandy debarked only to be greeted by a well-tanned man holding a sign that said Allen Tours. She waved at him as she made her way through the other passengers.

"Welcome to Palm Beach, Ms. Carlyle. I'm Fredrich Allen." Fredrich had a bright smile that showed through his dark tan. She deduced he was a robustly healthy man in his late fifties who spent a lot of time outdoors.

"Please call me Sandy," she said as she extended her hand. "I appreciate you meeting me personally. I read the manuscript on the way down and thoroughly enjoyed all that it contained."

"Glad you liked it. My wife and I kept records of our voyages over the years and thought it would be both a fun book and a good advertising piece. My wife, Linda, is out front waiting with the car. Did you check luggage?"

Sandy indicated she only had her carryon and then followed Fredrich out of the airport toward the waiting area. The warm Florida air touched her like a heavy blanket, yet felt remarkably comforting to her winter-weary body. Fredrich introduced her to his wife Linda, a delightful woman in her fifties, who also sported a perfect dark and healthy tan.

Heading from the airport, the Allen's exchanged information about their lives in Palm Beach along with the ups and downs of the charter business. Fredrich's father began the business about forty years ago when he returned from Navy duty. His father retired from the business, leaving it in the hands of Fredrich and Linda to operate.

Pulling into the parking lot at Allen Tours, Sandy immediately spotted the huge white boat at the end of the dock. "That is some big boat down there," she exclaimed. "Is that someone's private yacht?"

"That is our pride and joy, 'Eclipse,' who will provide safe passage for you during your time with us."

"I'm going to live on that boat?

Fredrick laughed. "We like to think of her as a ship or a yacht, but either way, that's your home for the duration. One of the reasons I wanted you down here to help us work on the book was to give you a real feel for the adventure of the water. No better way to do that than to take a trip on *Eclipse*."

Fredrich parked near *Eclipse*, giving Sandy time to truly embrace the magnificence of the ship. It appeared to be three stories high with a huge open deck in the back of both the main deck and the one above it. Fredrich and Linda guided Sandy down the ramp and onto the rear of the main deck.

"This is the lounge off the meeting room," Linda indicated, as they entered a large open area with several couches and a well-stocked bar. "The meeting area is for corporate charters who want to do some business. For pleasure cruises it doubles as a movie room and dance floor. The deck above us is for sun worshipers and the deck above that has the two lifeboats and the bridge. This deck has sleeping quarters for the crew plus two other guest rooms, and the deck above is the master suite, which will be your home, plus two other large bedrooms.

41

Captain's quarters are on the third deck. We'll get you settled in and then you can tour on your own."

Linda led her up a circular stairway to the sun deck and then down a hallway toward the front of the ship. Entering the room at the end of the hall, Sandy discovered a plush space containing a huge king-sized bed, two magnificent leather couches, a bar in the corner, and a dressing room off to the side. In the bathroom, there was a large whirlpool tub along with a spacious glass-enclosed shower, both of which faced a sizeable window overlooking the water.

"This is breathtaking," Sandy said quietly as she tried to take in the pure luxury of her surroundings.

"Our business is to make the wealthy and prosperous feel at home. It's not always easy, as they can often be very demanding, but generally, everyone who joins us has a great time. Why don't you get settled and then wander out to the rear deck on this floor. We'll be having dinner out there in about an hour."

After Linda left, Sandy stood in the middle of the room trying to take in the sheer lavishness of her surroundings. Looking over to the bathroom, she smiled, quickly threw off her clothes and hopped into the glass shower. Standing in the warm water looking out on the calm harbor, she felt like she was queen of the world. This was a journey into a fantasy world providing a wonderful break away from her very routine and boring existence. Feeling the water cascade over her naked body, Sandy decided that life just didn't get any better.

Chapter 6

Justin stood in the bridge going over the navigation equipment. The ship was top of the line in every aspect including one of the best autopilot devices he'd ever worked. With each new discovery, he actually felt pleasure coming back into his perceptions of life. The days he'd spent on his own boat ranked in the top of his memories. The last ten years drained his energy and time, leaving him a wealthy but unhappy man. In the last few hours on *Eclipse*, he felt like he'd regained ten years of life.

"Finding everything in order?"

Justin turned to see Fredrich enter the bridge carrying a box of some type.

"Fredrich, this is a piece of paradise. I feel like a kid in a candy store who doesn't know where to begin."

Fredrich set the box on the counter and smiled. "I know what you mean, and it's always fun for me to have someone else love her like I do." Sitting in the captain's chair, he looked over to Justin. "So, Justin Armond Betterly Jr., it appears you have quite a background. Don't know why you're trying to stay low-profile, but I'll keep the information on your background between you and me. Just promise me if you ever decide to take a charter down here you'll let me know. In the meantime, it will be a pleasure working with you."

"Thanks, Fredrich, I appreciate your keeping my confidentiality. I'm just tired of being accountable to everybody and want to drop out for a while."

"No problem," Fredrich said, sliding the box to Justin. "These are the charts for the island we cruise through when we take a short charter. I put a red tag on a couple that make for a nice cruise, but if you see anything you like better let me know. Our guest is aboard and we'll have dinner on the aft sundeck in about an hour."

Justin looked at the charts. "I'll take these to the aft deck and look through them. Think I understand how everything is set up on the bridge. How far are we going tonight?"

"Only about an hour off shore. Takes a half hour to get out to the ocean, and then we can run about ten miles out and hold up there. I'll run her tonight, so just relax and enjoy the ride. Did Linda show you to your suite?"

Justin laughed, "You put me in a pretty lavish room, I don't think it's crew quarters."

"Like I said," Fredrich replied, "if you ever want to charter down here, I want you to feel like this is the place you would come. Help yourself to a drink at the bar; you're off duty until tomorrow morning. We only have one passenger, so it will just be the four of us."

Justin picked up the folder, closed down the equipment he was using, and headed to the aft deck to look over the charts. Stopping at the bar, he fixed a drink with a beautiful bottle of Johnny Walker Black and then headed out into the Florida sunset. Spreading the charts on the table, he quickly grasped the inland water route that would take them to the Lake Worth channel to the Atlantic Ocean. The *Eclipse* needed a lot of space to move free, however he knew the boat was well equipped with bow and aft thrusters for quick course correction. The trip Fredrich earmarked took them toward the Bimini Islands but appeared to move into some of the smaller reef islands to the north. Weather permitting it would be an easy and beautiful cruise.

"Hello, mind if I join you?"

Glancing up from the charts, Justin was caught off guard by the woman standing near him. He was no stranger to women; he usually felt comfortable and confident in their presence. However, something about this particular female caught him by surprise. She was average height with a solid athletic build, yet her bright green eyes seemed to send energy to him that was almost palpable. Realizing he was staring at her, he stood and extended his hand. "Please join me, I was lost in thought and I guess you surprised me. I'm Justin."

Firmly grasping his outstretched hand, Sandy introduced herself and took a seat next to him at the table. Looking at the charts she asked, "Are you the ship's navigator?"

Straightening up his pile of charts, Justin leaned back and once again felt the strange reaction this woman gave him. "I'm part navigator, part pilot, and part whatever Fredrich has in mind. I just signed on for this cruise because his other crew was out sick. Can I fix you a drink?"

"That would be great. If they have vodka and cranberry, I would love it." Sandy watched as Justin went to the bar to fill her request. He was an attractive man with dark hair and a trim build. She guessed he was around forty-five, but she could never really tell with men. He seemed ill at ease in their brief conversation but might have been surprised by her showing up while he was studying. Setting the drink before her, she did note the absence of a wedding ring, but again, that didn't always mean he wasn't married.

"So where is this magnificent ship heading, Justin? I guess I'll be happy no matter where it goes, it's an overwhelming place to be."

"She is a beauty. I just happened to be admiring her when Fredrich came by. It ended up he needed help, and I had the experience he desired, so it all worked out well. I wanted to see the ship up close, and this is as close as you can get. To answer your question, it appears Fredrich intends to head toward the Bimini Islands, which lay off the coast about sixty miles. Probably stay in that area for a couple days and then head back to port. Have you ever been here before?"

"I've been down to Miami but can't say it was my favorite trip. Nice city, but not my kind of place. Other than that, no real experience in Florida. Are you from around here?"

"No, just passing through. Spent some time in Miami but much like you, I decided it wasn't for me. Is this a vacation trip on the *Eclipse* or business?" Justin wanted to steer the conversation away from his life and back on to her. He was just a hired worker on the ship and wanted to leave it that way. He listened as she explained about her purpose for being on board, her job in

New York, and other facts that made conversation with her very easy. She'd pulled her dark hair back in a ponytail that gave her a very relaxed and youthful look, yet she remained a very confident and self-assured person. She had on a short, sporty skirt that complimented her well-toned legs. Her light blouse flattered her breasts, which definitely appeared to not be encumbered with a brassiere. After so many shallow and plastic women in his life, he found Sandy to be a fresh breath of air.

"I see you two found each other," Linda called out as she entered from the hall holding a large tray with several dishes. Justin met her and helped set the tray on the table. "I brought up the salad and some munchies to get started until Freddy does something magic on the bar-b-que. Let me get a drink and then join you. Help yourself to the food."

Sandy set plates at four chairs and placed the salad bowl in the middle. It was hard to believe she was sitting on a luxury yacht in Palm Beach Florida and feeling like it was a place she belonged. Linda was a big help as she was one of those people who made a party fun. In addition, Justin was a fascinating person who was a good conversationalist as well as a handsome man. He did seem rather reluctant to disclose much information, but men who work on ships may be that way. For her, the bottom line clearly demonstrated this trip was fantastic.

Dinner was a treat with great grilled steaks. Fredrich and Linda shared about the business, and the laughs they had over the years, enabling Sandy to understand that Allen Tours wasn't just a business it was a passion they shared together. They'd been married for twenty-eight years, had no children, and loved the ability to travel as they pleased. The dinner gave Sandy even more insight on how to structure the book so it would capture all the Allens' desired.

After dinner, Sandy and Linda cleaned up, as the two men prepared to get under way. Once clear of the dock, Fredrich told Justin to go enjoy life and if anything came up where he was needed, he would call him.

After fixing another drink, Justin headed to the main deck and found the two women watching the last rays of the sunset. The ship moved quietly along the intercostal as it headed for the Lake Worth channel; not making a sound other than the quiet splash of water on the hull. They had another drink together and then Linda said she had to go keep Fredrich company so he didn't get lonely. She indicated they would go to anchor in about an hour or so. Breakfast would be around eight a.m. when they would continue their journey.

She showed Justin how to turn on the music, and he found some quiet steel drum songs he and Sandy believed were appropriate for the night. Fixing another

drink, they settled in lounge chairs
watching the last light of day fade away.

"I can see why a person would fall
in love with being at sea," Sandy said
quietly as she relaxed in the calm of the
night. "This is heaven on earth."

"It isn't always like this.
Nevertheless, the good does outweigh the
bad," Justin replied.

Looking over to Justin she asked,
"Do you work on the ships all the time,
or is this just a part time thing?"

Justin tensed for a minute, unsure
of how to handle the question and then
decided to make it a partial truth. "I've
worked on enough boats it could be full
time if I wanted, but I usually don't
stay in one place long enough to make it
a career. I've worked a ship similar to
this in the Pacific, so being on this one
is easy even if it's larger."

Leaning back, Sandy reflected, "I'd
love to be able to pick up and go
wherever I wanted, but I never mastered

the art of being unemployed. I started my business with the thought I'd have more free time, but it went the opposite way with more demands and less freedom."

Justin smiled, thinking about the last ten years and how they had literally trapped him. "I know what you mean. I've been in that type of trap but finally decided life was too short to keep doing what other people want. Sometimes you just have to do what you want in the moment and not worry about tomorrow. I plan on finding out how that works over the next one hundred years."

They both laughed and then relaxed into a comfortable silence as the music changed into a slower beat. Looking at Sandy, Justin asked, "Would you like to seize this moment and dance?"

"Thank you, kind sir, I do believe I would like that." Sandy stood and realized she was a little tipsy, and it wasn't because she was on the water. Too much Vodka and too much fun! Then she decided there wasn't any rule that said you couldn't have too much fun. The beauty of the *Eclipse* gave the illusion that life had no problems. If something wasn't to your liking, ring a bell and the world would be changed to fit your desires. She looked at Justin as he stood to dance and decided that this moment everything in the world was just what she wanted.

Taking Sandy into his arms, Justin felt a comfort he had long missed. The smell of her hair and the touch of her hand sent a spark that surprised him. Pulling Sandy a little tighter, he confirmed that his original assumption of no bra was correct, causing even more electricity to surge through his body. Over the last months, his free time was spent with accountants, lawyers, buyout experts, and other leaches that drained him, leaving no time for pleasure. He'd had a couple opportunities for one-night stands but was tired of fake people;

especially fake women who'd suck his dick and empty his wallet at the same time.

"What are you thinking, Justin?" Sandy asked as she looked up at him. "You seem quiet."

"I guess I'm just enjoying the moment. I have to admit, I'm also enjoying holding you. It's been a while since I danced and liked it."

Sandy leaned in closer to Justin, resting her head on his shoulder. When she'd finished her shower, the desire to feel unencumbered overwhelmed her, so she chose to go braless for the night assuming she wouldn't be with anyone who might notice. In her somewhat uninhibited state of mind, she'd forgotten about that decision until Justin held her close. Her sensitive nipples touched his chest as he held her, causing a tingle to run through her breasts, finding a direct path right between her legs. Now his leg was pressing lightly between hers, and she thought she might come unglued and attack him right there.

This was ridiculous; she was a hired consultant for Allen Tours, not some tourist who came on their boat to make out with the help. Deciding she needed to make some space between them, she pulled back and looked at him. As she did, he leaned closer and kissed her. Unsure for a second, she hesitated until her natural needs took over, and she kissed him back.

Drawing her close, Justin felt her full breasts press into his chest, as her lips parted, allowing their tongues to explore each other. There was a hunger in her that touched the desire in him, giving him courage to slide his hand down her back until he felt the edge of her blouse. Slipping his fingers below the fabric, he caressed the warmth and softness of her flesh. Her breath shortened as she pulled him closer, pressing her throbbing nipples into his chest. Kissing him passionately, Sandy placed her hand on his and pulled it to her naked breast. Lightly running his fingers over the softness of her skin, he cupped his hand around her and squeezed, feeling its richness and warmth. Sensing her erect nipple burrowing into his palm, he moved his hand and rubbed its hardness between his thumb and finger.

Sandy felt the current run from her nipple and explode through her body. Justin released her nipple and surrounded her tingling breast with his hand, massaging it gently as he pressed it against her ribcage. She felt his other hand pull her to him, allowing her abdomen to feel the hardness in his pants. Pulling back, she ran her fingers down his body and put her hand on his as he gently massaged her breast.

Breathlessly, she looked into his blue eyes and smiled. "I guess this is what we call seizing the moment."

He kissed her and quietly said, "If what I'm seizing is called the moment, I can't wait to find out what the other one is called."

Laughing quietly, she reached to her blouse and slowly undid the buttons until it hung loose over her body. Justin released her breast and parted her shirt on both sides until it slid over her shoulders and down to the middle of her back. Brushing his fingers on her neck, he kissed her as he gently moved over her shoulder, down her chest and onto her extended breasts. Stepping back, he continued to caress both breasts while looking into her misty-green eyes. "You are a very beautiful woman, Sandy."

She laughed softly, continuing to feel the ecstasy flowing through her body as he touched her. "I bet you say that to all the naked women you find."

Justin smiled. "No, believe me when I tell you that's not just some standard line. You are truly a beautiful woman, and I mean it."

Feeling like she was going to
explode in her skin, she took his hand
and turned to the stairway to her suite.
"Let's go find out if you really mean
it."

Chapter 7

Pulling Sandy close, Justin shut the door to her suite. "I really don't want to do anything that you'll regret later."

"I appreciate that, but I think we're both over twenty-one and reasonably in control of our senses," Sandy said quietly as she stepped back. "Besides, I said I wanted to see if you really meant it and the only way to answer that question is to reveal the entire package." Saying this, she slipped the shirt off her shoulders allowing it to fall to the ground. Justin gazed with appreciation at the semi-naked woman before him who now exposed her beautifully filled-out breasts and trim waist. Drawing her close, he kissed her deeply as his hands moved to touch the warmth of her skin.

Sandy felt the excitement develop once more as she started to unbutton Justin's shirt, desperately wanting to feel flesh on flesh. Moving his hands from her breasts, he shrugged off his shirt, revealing a muscular frame. With a deep groan, she pushed her breasts into his chest, kissing him intensely as currents of passion wracked her body. Her nipples screamed in delight as she pressed into his chest hair, slid over his flesh, and then backed up so he could easily grasp them.

Slowly they moved toward the king-sized bed kissing, fondling and surrendering to each other's touch. Tumbling onto the bed, Justin pulled Sandy close, taking her breast in his mouth. As Justin drew her hard nipple into his mouth, Sandy groaned with delight, moving her position to allow a repeat action on her other side.

Rolling her onto her back, Justin's hands slid down her waist until they contacted her skirt. He continued to pull her nipples deep in his mouth as his hand pressed on the skirt and embraced the growing passion between her legs. Reaching lower, he grasped her inner thigh, as she slowly spread her legs to his touch. Opening his hand, Justin extended his fingers and leisurely moved up her thigh until he discovered Sandy was not only braless, she was totally naked under her skirt. Progressing further, he felt the heat of her body increase under his fingers until he touched her open and moist vaginal lips. Running his hand over her, he caressed the softness of skin and knew Sandy was smooth and shaved, without a trace of hair. Spreading her lips, he slowly moved his fingers into her as she grasped him tightly in her arms, breathing rapidly.

His fingers hit a spot in her that made her stomach tighten into a ball. She knew the feeling and groaned breathlessly, "Justin, I'm losing it. I am going to explode." Sitting up on his elbow, he moved his fingers deeper. "Open your eyes and look at me as you climax. I want to watch you."

Forcing her eyes open, she peered into his dark blue eyes as her frenzy rose rapidly to the surface. Unable to wait, she grasped her breast and still looking into his eyes, exploded in a volcano of ecstasy. Pulling her close, he squeezed her throbbing pussy tight and held her as she experienced wave after wave of release until she finally relaxed in his arms. Removing his hand from between her legs, he caressed her glistening breasts covered in light perspiration and then kissed her neck. "Are you feeling better?"

Murmuring quietly into his shoulder she sighed, "More than words can express." Her satisfaction overshadowed her surprise that she had so rapidly fallen into bed with this stranger. Nevertheless, the feeling of his hands on her body provided enough information that she really couldn't classify him as a stranger. Running her hand through his hair, as he touched her breasts and kissed her neck, she felt the desire to continue the night's activities.

Slipping her hand down his neck, she stroked the hair on his chest, feeling the strength in his upper body along with the rapid heartbeat beneath. Continuing to move her hand down to his waist, she reached past the band of his shorts, grasped his swollen erection, and massaged it lightly. Gliding out of his grasp, Sandy reached down to undo Justin's shorts, freeing his erection for greater exploration. Seizing it in both hands, she felt a passion rip through her body setting off a desire designed to throw her out of control. How long had it been since she had touched a hard dick? Way too long, she decided as she moved

down his body embracing his hardness with
her mouth.

The warmth of her mouth on his
throbbing cock almost brought forth an
explosion, which Justin was able to
control, at least for the moment.
Reaching over, he drew her body over his
face, pushed up her skirt and spread her
legs over his chest. As she continued to
embrace his erection, he drew her close,
ran his fingers over her glittering
pussy, parted her lips and penetrated her
with his tongue, tasting the fruit of her
last orgasm.

Sandy felt the movement within her
and pulled hard on the swollen member now
deep in her mouth. She experienced Justin
moving his tongue through the folds of
her vagina as he explored every crevice
while working his way up to her erect and
sensitive clit. She was rapidly sliding
toward the edge of the orgasmic cliff
when she tasted the first salty release
of his cum.

Justin was losing it and couldn't hold back. He was about to pull away when he felt Sandy take him deeper into her mouth as she continued to slide her hand up and down the shaft. Knowing he was about to explode, he pulled Sandy's wetness into his mouth and pressed his tongue directly on her clit. He tasted her cum as she began to trickle over his tongue until she pressed hard on him and burst into an orgasmic torrent, which ran down on his chest.

His erection was throbbing in her mouth, as she stroked him harder and faster. The explosion rocketed through her body causing her to suck tightly on Justin, as he erupted deep in her throat. Sucking on him, she enjoyed the tension in his body as she completed her own orgasmic delight.

At last, she rolled off of Justin and lay on her back catching her breath. She sensed him sit up and apparently remove his shorts. He then left the bed, but she was too spent to even see where he was going. Finally curious about his absence, she rolled to her side, discovering he was no longer in the room. About to stand, she saw him exit the bathroom with two glasses and a towel in his hand.

"Sorry, had trouble finding the vodka and cranberry up here, so you get vodka and tonic." Handing her the glass, he indicated she should lie back on the pillows. Complying with his wishes, she watched as he reached down and finally slid off her well-wrinkled skirt. Spreading her legs, he placed the warm towel between them and softly washed her still sensitive garden.

"Did I drown you when I came?" she asked.

"Not as much as I drowned you. Nevertheless, I loved every moment. You're a beautiful woman Sandy, not only sexually, but overall."

Setting the towel on the floor, he took his drink and settled next to Sandy as she leaned on his arm. "Thanks Justin, you too, sir, are a gentleman and a beautiful lover. I haven't done that for a while, but I'm very happy we did it tonight. I think the *Eclipse* must have some type of aphrodisiac in the water that gave me the ability to really relax and enjoy myself. Thank you."

Looking into his beautiful blue eyes, she raised her glass. "Carpe Diem; here's to seizing the moment."

Returning her toast with his glass he replied, "And doing it every day for one hundred years."

Chapter 8

The morning sun poured through the large portals over Sandy's bed stirring her out of beautiful dreams. Reaching for her watch on the nightstand, she realized the bed was larger than normal, forcing her to search her foggy memory until she recalled being on the Allens' yacht someplace out in the Atlantic Ocean. The watch indicated it was seven thirty in the morning, allowing her to settle back into the comfort and luxury surrounding her without the necessity of rushing out to work. The satin sheets on her naked flesh stirred her memory of last night's sexual escapade with Justin.

Looking over to the table, she saw the two glasses from the night before still mostly full of liquid. She

remembered lying naked with him talking,
although she had no memory of falling
asleep. She assumed she drifted off, and
he removed the drinks to the table, then
left for his own suite. It was probably
the correct gesture; nevertheless, she
wished she could have woken in his arms
this morning. Throwing back the covers,
she ran her hands down her naked frame
allowing the touch and memory to combine
as she once again entered into the
passionate recollection of last night.
His touch awakened a desire within her
that she had forgotten. It was more than
the sexual connection, which was perfect
in so many ways; it was a harmony with
another person taking place in a safe and
secure moment. The problem was, she
didn't know Justin well enough to truly
discern if he was either safe or secure.
Nevertheless, for the moment they shared
last night, he was all she needed.

Now comes the awkward part. 'The
morning after the night before.' She had

no regrets about their sexual activity, hoped he felt the same. However, it wasn't like they could wave goodbye and disappear; they were on a boat in the middle of the ocean. One thing was certain, Justin was not only a gentle and fantastic lover, he was simply a very nice man. True, she didn't know anything about him; he may be a serial killer for all she knew, but somehow she really believed he was a decent person. He obviously was a drifter without any real roots, but that was also part of his attraction.

Sandy wondered how a person could live a life without any direction or purpose. Maybe that was her problem; she'd always been the conscientious one who stayed the course and fixed all the errors around her. Not that she regretted her life; she loved her work and friends, but she always wondered what it would be like to live like Justin seemed to live.

Slipping out of the luxury of her bed and heading to the bathroom, she hesitated at the door to look at the luxurious room surrounding her. This may not be her life, but for the next few days, she would enjoy it and maybe do some of it with Justin. Smiling, she raised her hand and cried out, "Carpe Diem."

Justin sipped his coffee as he scanned the dials before him. *Eclipse* actually ran herself if you left her alone, but the little boy in him enjoyed playing captain of the magnificent ship. He and Fredrich set course around six thirty that morning, and then Fredrich went below to check on the engines and help Linda with breakfast.

Looking out at the blue-green waters surrounding him, Justin felt like he'd been born anew. As far as the eye could see there was nothing but water, which was the home for more life that anyone

74

could imagine. Not a deeply spiritual man, he always felt awestruck by the balance of life in the ocean. Not only was it endless with life, it was the source of life itself, providing water for the land it surrounded.

Sipping his coffee, he flipped on the autopilot and stepped out on the bridge deck so he could smell the air. The freshness of it reminded him of the smell of Sandy's hair, which brought back the memory of last night. How they ended up naked in bed was a journey he could hardly reconstruct, but one he definitely enjoyed. Sandy was a beautiful, sexy, and fun woman who seemed to genuinely enjoy life. However, she was also a guest on a ship he was supposedly working on, thus causing him a little concern as to how she might feel about last night. When she fell asleep, he sat for about a half hour just looking at her. Justin prided himself on being in control of his emotions and desires, yet this woman had impacted him from the time he laid eyes on her.

As she lay sleeping, he was enamored not only with her nakedness, but the sense of contentment she seemed to carry both awake and asleep. Thinking about his own life, Justin wondered what it would be like to simply be happy with who you were. Looking out over the water, he decided he had no idea, but would make a note to himself to try to discover the answer.

Justin found Linda and Fredrich on the aft deck of the second floor, setting a table for breakfast. "What can I do to help?" he asked.

"You can freshen my coffee and then have a seat," Linda said as she set a plate of eggs and bacon on the table. "There's ice tea on the bar if you want that instead."

"Good morning, everyone. What a beautiful day."

Justin turned at the sound of her voice and felt his face flush, as she looked directly at him.

"Hi Justin, did you get up early and get this beautiful ship moving?"

"Fredrich and I got her moving, but she has a will of her own, so we decided to just let her run herself."

Sandy's eyes opened wide. "You mean nobody is steering *Eclipse*?"

Justin smiled, "She has an autopilot that runs her. If radar picks up something she can't avoid, she shuts down and signals us. You look well today. Did you sleep okay last night?"

Smiling at him, she touched his arm lightly. "I slept better than I have in a long time."

Linda entered and gave Sandy a hug. "Have a seat, honey, and eat before it all gets cold. How did you sleep last night? It was a calm sea, but sometimes it takes a while to get used to the motion of the ship."

"Last night was perfect in every way possible. You're really spoiling me." Sandy laughed as she took some eggs and bacon. "When would you and Fredrich like to go over some of my notes on the book?"

Fredrich sat at the table saying, "We have a good two hours before any activity on board so why don't we work after breakfast. Justin, the port engine is a little rough today. Can you check the carburetor and see if you see any problem? We can run on starboard for a while."

"No problem," Justin said. "I've been anxious to go see them in action."

The four of them chatted their way through breakfast without any references to last night. As they parted after breakfast Justin and Sandy locked eyes, smiled, and then went their separate ways.

Sandy gathered with the Allens at the conference desk on the main deck. The doors to the deck were open, allowing the delightful sea breeze to flow into the cabin. Sandy went over her notes about some structure questions, also reviewing certain grammatical changes she wanted to make. At last, she leaned back looking at both of them. "So that's the easy part of the book. What is it you really want me to accomplish here, because I don't think it's just editing."

Fredrich looked at Linda. "We need a miracle?"

Linda laughed, "Not a miracle per say, but definitely something that will open doors we need to reach. Allen Tours has six yachts in its fleet, the largest being this *Eclipse*. Four of the boats are paid in full, one is almost paid off but this one is highly mortgaged by the bank. The economy has fallen off and it's difficult to charter out all the fleet. We've decided to sell off three of the fleet so we can reduce the debt on *Eclipse*, but that also means we've lost some revenue-producing charters. We need to sell the concept of luxury charter on *Eclipse* as a life-changing experience. The stories in the book are all true, and everyone involved in the stories provided permission for us to use them. The names of the celebrities will definitely help in marketing, but we need something that will stir people and make them want to come aboard. Not everybody can afford it, but those who can need to be on *Eclipse*."

Sandy sat quietly for a minute. "I'm a little concerned. I'm an editor, not a writer. I rework what other people write, not create my own pieces."

Fredrich reached into a box and slid something across the table. Sandy picked it up and let out a short gasp. "Where did you get this?"

"Your friend John Rawlings gave it to us about a year ago," Linda said.

Sandy looked at the book and read the title: *"Heartbeat, a love story by Sandra Carlyle Booth."*

In the early days of her marriage Sandy wrote two books, both love stories, neither very popular. Her husband, asshole that he was, told her she was a bad writer and shouldn't waste her time. The publisher was prepared to spend some money to get the books out, but Sandy believed her husband and decided she was just an editor not a writer.

"How did John get this?" she asked quietly.

"For that question I have no answer, " Linda said, "but what's in your book is why you're here. John's a good friend and is well aware of our financial situation with the company. Over the years, we've shared a lot of stories together, and he recommended we put them in a book. Then he gave us yours and said when we were ready to put it together, you were the person to call. I read your book and fell in love with it. You are a beautiful writer, and we want to have your touch in our book.

Sandy set the book on the table and stared at it. She felt her throat tighten, then lost control, and began to cry. Excusing herself, she went to the bar in order to find some paper towels. When she turned, Linda was standing before her.

"Somebody stabbed you in your creative spot didn't they?" Linda said as she put her arms around Sandy. Holding her tight, Sandy began to sob in ways she hadn't allowed in years. Linda just held her until the sobs began to subside.

"I'm sorry," Sandy said as she wiped her eyes on the towel, "I just hadn't visited that place in years. I guess I stuffed it deep. You're right Linda, my ex-husband stabbed me in my creative place and in my heart. I guess I decided if I buried it, then I could avoid the pain. I've wanted to be a writer ever since I was a little girl. All the way through college, people told me I could write. Then I married this miserable man who proceeded to destroy every confidence I possessed. He cheated on me during the honeymoon and convinced me it was my fault. He destroyed me to keep me under his thumb. It was my last ounce of courage that finally gave me strength to divorce him. I've spent the last years regaining who I was, but until just now I never thought about being a writer again. I don't know if I can do it and you have so much riding on this book."

"Sandy, one thing Linda and I do know about is loving," Fredrich said. "We are one in every way because we choose to love each other as a primary responsibility, not as an afterthought. Reading your book, we knew you felt the same way about life. You may have been beaten up a little, but you're a woman who knows about loving. You stir that up, spend time on *Eclipse*, and let's see what happens."

Sandy went to both of them and gave them a hug. Smiling, with tears in her eyes, she said, "Carpe Diem."

Chapter 9

Wiping grease off his hands, Justin exited the engine room. Hitting the start button, he listened as the port engine began to rotate. Soon its hum was in harmony with the starboard side, sounding like a deep-voiced male chorus in an opera. He smiled; that was one of the dumber analogies he'd come up with in several years. When he started thinking thoughts that dumb, he knew he was relaxing.

"Justin, you down there?"

"Yeah, Sandy, hang on I'll be right up."

"No, wait," she said, as he heard her footsteps on the stairs. "I want to see the engines that drive this goddess."

Stepping into the light of the engine room, Sandy looked somehow different. She still had that beautiful smile, but her presence seemed softer.

"Whew, it's warmer down here," she said. "How long have you been here?"

Sandy couldn't help but notice that Justin had thrown off his shirt and his muscular frame now glistened in the heat of the lower deck.

"I guess about an hour, but I found the problem and was heading up. Want to see the engines?"

Nodding yes, Sandy followed Justin into the rear section of the lower deck. The heat and noise were powerful, but the space was immaculate enough to eat off the floor. She could feel the power of the twin motors, and their rhythm sent ripples through her body. Turning, she looked at Justin with a sly smile, drew him close and embraced him. Feeling the warmth of her body, he kissed her saying, "Let's go where it's quieter and cooler."

"In a minute," she said as she again slyly smiled at him. Stepping back from his embrace, she reached down and pulled her shirt over her head. Standing naked from the waist up, she leaned toward him. "Now kiss me like I'm a deck hand below deck, all sweaty and hot."

Justin laughed as he swept her into his arms and held her tight. Her body felt cool on his flesh as her breasts slid across his sweaty chest. Kissing her deeply, she dropped into his embrace, feeling his arms hold her tightly as she pressed her groin into his rapidly hardening cock. Her breathing became more intense as she spread her legs, allowing more space for his hardness to press against as they embraced. She lifted her mouth to his ear, "Will you fuck me here? I want you so much. Fuck me hard."

Turning her back to him, she reached up and held onto a bar running through the engine room. Her naked back reacted to the hot engine room and glistened with sweat. Justin came up behind her and grabbed her breasts with both hands, as she stretched her arms up to the pipe over her head. Sliding his hands down her body he pulled off her shorts and kicked them aside. His fingers descended to her ass, which quivered as he grasped it firmly. Pulling her tightly to his body, he moved his hand around her and dropped his fingers between her legs. Rubbing her lips, he felt her spread her legs further apart giving room for him to explore the depth of her heat and moisture. Moving his other hand up her body, he sensed the perspiration between her breasts and on her neck.

Releasing his grip, he reached up, grasped her hands on the bar and pulled them down, placing them in front of her on the lower step of the ladder. As she bent over before him he dragged down his shorts and grasped her ass, pulling her cheeks apart. Bending closer to the floor, her movement revealed the wet, pink cavern beckoning to be explored.

Placing his hard cock on her, he pushed in, penetrating quickly and deeply. He heard her moan as he plunged, feeling her push back against him, driving him deeper. "Go, go, take me now," she hollered above the engine noise. Grabbing her ass, he began to pound on her, driving harder and deeper with each stroke. Sweat poured from his body and splashed on her back and ass. Gripping the ladder step, she bent over as far as she could, providing an open target for his pounding dick.

Meeting her thrusts with his own, Justin felt Sandy become tight inside. Pushing harder, he reach around, grabbed her breasts, and squeezed them, as he felt her shatter in passion. Pushing one more time, he pulled out of her and began to climax. Sandy spun and grabbed his hard cock, holding it against her breasts as he ejaculated. Grasping the ladder to steady himself, he watched as Sandy collapsed to the floor. She looked up at him from her seated position and smiled. Reaching down he pulled her up, handing her a clean towel from the workbench. She wiped the sweat off his body and then off her breasts.

Kissing him, she leaned into his ear and said, "Thanks, you follow directions well." Handing her the clothes she had thrown to the floor, he smacked her naked ass and pointed to the door. "Let's go cool down for a minute. You are wearing me out, but I couldn't be happier."

Stopping in the coolness of the stairway outside the engine room, Justin pulled on his shirt, as Sandy adjusted her shorts and t-shirt. "So what was that all about, other than being a fun time?" he asked her.

Pulling her sweaty hair back into a ponytail, Sandy laughed. "I guess it was a pent up desire to escape into fantasy, or maybe you just turn me on so much I can't resist you. I'm a little surprised at the intensity of how I felt; can't say I ever demanded to be fucked before, but it was what I wanted and what you provided was totally in harmony with my desire."

Justin brushed some loose hair from her face. "I guess this means you have no regrets about last night."

"Well, in all honesty, I do have a regret," she said, smiling. "I wished I had stayed awake so we could have done it again. Nevertheless, the 'boiler-room bang' we just had was a good follow-up."

After going to their individual suites to clean up, Justin took Sandy up to the bridge to show her the navigation system of *Eclipse*. Fredrich was sitting at a table reviewing a chart, while the ship continued on its course untouched by human hands. "Hey, you two, are you up for civilization or for tropical rustic? We can head to Bimini, which is an island paradise all by itself, or we can go a little north to some of the islands that are uninhabited yet beautiful."

"I'm happy just to be onboard, Captain," Sandy said, "so it's your choice as far as I'm concerned.

"Same here." Justin said as he took a quick look at the instrument panel.

"Okay," said Fredrich as he looked up smiling, "then we'll do it my way and see both. Let's do rustic first. Justin, reset the course for 160 degrees and lets go see paradise."

Justin set the direction, as he leaned over to Sandy and quietly said, "I think I just saw paradise in the engine room." Sandy laughed and punched Justin's shoulder, as Fredrich sat behind them watching and smiling broadly.

Linda and Sandy enjoyed a beautiful sunny day on the aft section of the main deck. Sandy was proud she no longer called it the 'back of the ship' but now correctly referred to it as the 'aft.'

Sipping some kind of drink Linda made in a blender, Sandy looked at her and said, "I'm sorry I lost it when we met today, but I really do appreciate you being there as I spilled my past sorrows on your beautiful table."

"Honey, believe me, that isn't the worst thing that's been spilt on that table. One thing I've learned in this business is to be a good listener. People think if you just have enough money, then life is all a bed of roses. No doubt money can help, but I've seen some miserable people that have more money than God. What you accumulate in life doesn't count as much as what you believe about yourself. When we bought *Eclipse*, we knew it was a big risk. We could have lived on what we were making and not had a worry, but something in us said it was too early in life to take it easy, so let's live the adventure. Even if it doesn't work, we at least believed enough to try. If you do that, somehow you'll always end up on your feet."

Sandy sipped her drink as she listened to the truth of Linda's words. "I know you're right. I always believed I'd be able to be a writer and find happiness in simply creating. When I met my ex, somehow I gave control of my life to him. He was a jerk, but it was my choice to give in, and I followed that choice. My therapist said I was looking to fulfill my father's abandonment. Probably true, as he left my mom when I was about six, and he never returned. After I divorced, I took time to repair myself mentally and physically. I guess what I hit this morning was a part I haven't worked on yet."

Linda turned toward Sandy. "You have to prioritize yourself in this journey, or you'll lose it to someone else. Doesn't mean you have to be selfish and nasty to people, just means you have to be conscious of what you're doing and figure out if it is really what you want to do. If not, don't do it."

"You said before: it is choices. That thought's been my saving outlook for the last few years. I could have been a victim and blamed my ex for my miserable life, but I decided to take responsibility for my own actions. I chose to be with him and lose who I was. Now I choose not to be with him and live my own life. I guess that's what you mean by taking care of my journey."

Leaning back, Linda looked over at Sandy. "Life is good, honey. Life is real good. Use it wisely, share it with those who respect you, and then enjoy the ride."

Lifting her glass, Sandy said, "Here's to the ride."

Linda clicked glasses with her and smiled. "To the ride."

Chapter 10

Sandy stood next to Fredrich, as he navigated the ship around a small island and set course for one that was further ahead. "Hardest things about this area are the shoals below the waterline," he said as he pointed to a screen showing their depth and a shadow image of the water around them. "The charts show the general depth, but a strong storm can change the depth by two or three feet, and that's not something we need to stumble into with a ship this size. We need at least a five-foot clearance and some of these go up to four feet. Most of the time, we operate in water that's a couple hundred feet deep but not back in these reefs.

Fredrich moved the Eclipse past the small island, and Sandy saw the depth go from ten feet to fifty in a few seconds. "Is that the island we're heading toward?" she asked, pointing to the long island far before them.

"No, that's North Bimini, and we'll head there later. There are small islands near here that aren't populated but offer tremendous reefs for diving and snorkeling. We'll anchor out here and take an inflatable into the shore. It's much too shallow to bring *Eclipse* in close. Justin and Linda are on the lower aft deck getting it ready for the trip. You and Justin getting along okay?"

Sandy hesitated for a second, unsure how to respond as Justin was Fredrich's employee, and she didn't want him to be in trouble. "He's been very helpful showing me around the ship and explaining how things operate. I appreciate his help."

Fredrich laughed. "Sandy, you don't have to protect his job. I'm happy as long as you're happy. If you two want to spend time together, who am I to define how you spend that time? Relax on this trip, feel the real passion of being on *Eclipse,* and enjoy the cruise. You'll write about that experience, not the navigation equipment. Besides, Justin is just with me for this trip, although I wish I could talk him into more."

Sandy smiled as she looked at Fredrich, realizing he was well aware of the relationship between her and Justin. Fredrich and Linda may not know all that she and Justin had done, but they were smart enough to know it wasn't just sitting around talking sports. "I guess he just drifts from place to place," she said. "He doesn't disclose much about himself when we talk."

"There's always a lot we never know about other people," Fredrich said as he slowed the ship off the shore of the island. "Sometimes it's just better to take them for what they present and not dig too deep. Only thing I can tell you about Justin is his record is clean without any criminal activity. Little I've seen of him, he's a decent guy in search of life."

Dropping anchor, Fredrich secured the deck and waved for Sandy to follow him down the stairs. "Lets go see what paradise has to offer us today. I think you'll enjoy it."

On the main deck's aft section, they found Linda and Justin placing coolers into a large inflatable boat. Linda waved to her. "Hey, girl, let's go for a ride. Jump in as we lower this thing."

Sandy stepped into the boat, finding a seat in the middle next to Linda. Fredrich motioned Justin to get in the front of the boat, and then he started an electric winch, lowering them into the water. He climbed aboard as he and Justin released the lines. Fredrich started a small motor, while Linda explained about their destination.

"This is a great area of reefs and shoals which make for perfect diving experience. The little island we're heading toward is uninhabited but makes a perfect location to use for snorkeling." She pointed toward a large land mass off to the right. "That's North Bimini and is part of the Bahamas' chain of islands. We'll sail around it later."

Sandy looked over the edge of the raft, amazed at the clear water and the array of colors they contained. Watching as Fredrich wove his way toward their destination, she saw thousands of different fish darting around the rocks and coral masses. They pulled up on the beach area where they secured the raft. Hauling out several sets of snorkel equipment, Linda handed them out to everybody and then explained the plan. "We'll go in on the shallow waters until you get familiar with the equipment. Stay away from the deep red coral, as it's sharp. Also, don't stick your hands into any of the rock or coral crevices; you might end up with a painful bite. Other than that, have a blast."

Having explained this, she headed toward the water, and the others followed. Sandy finally got her swim fins on and started out into the water. Justin stayed close to her as they explored the beauty of the natural life around them. Sandy was entranced with the small fish that seemed to number in the hundreds, watching as they all moved in one direction, and then on some unspoken cue completely changed directions. Rounding a corner, she came face to face with a fish that had a huge nose. Pulling back, she surfaced with a shock, as Justin wrapped an arm around her and laughed.

"That's a parrot fish and it's completely safe." He laughed, " I'm sure you scared him more than he did you."

Sandy relaxed in Justin's arms and floated on the beautiful salt water. "This place is paradise," she whispered softly. "I can see how people move here and never leave."

"This area is a lot like the Australian outer reef area, but the fish here are smaller. In the Australian area you run into sharks, although we probably would find the same things here if we went out a little further."

"No thanks, I like it here," Sandy said, pulling closer to Justin. "Sharks are not what I want to see today or any day. Especially if they're up close."

They turned when they heard Linda in the distance. "Come on in, you two. It's chow time."

They swam back to the beach, finding Linda and Fredrich near some tropical trees providing shade from the hot midday sun. They'd unpacked a feast of fresh seafood salad and rolls, which they all easily devoured.

"Linda and I are going back to the boat for a while," Fredrich explained after they finished lunch. "We have a call to make back to the office which will only take about a half hour. You can come with us or just stay here and explore."

Sandy looked over at Justin, "I'd love to stay a little longer if it's okay with you."

"You don't have to ask twice," he said.

"Okay," Fredrich said, "I'll leave one of the ship-to-shore radios so we can let you know if we're running late, and you can also contact us if you need anything. We'll be gone about two hours round-trip."

They all piled things into the raft and then Fredrich and Linda pushed off toward the ship. *Eclipse* looked like a beautiful white castle as she sat in the distance surrounded by the vivid blue waters.

Sandy turned to Justin. "Want to go in the water or explore the island?"

"Given the size of the island, we can probably do both," he said, "so let's start with ground exploration."

Stopping long enough to slip on some shoes, they entered the tree line on the beach where it was shady and comfortable. Slightly worn pathways indicated others had explored the little island before them, so Justin and Sandy decided to stay on the path and see where it took them. The island wasn't thick with tropical trees, but it did provide an array of flowers along with a few pesky insects. The path led to a dense place in the trees, forcing them to stoop low in order to enter the clearing beyond. On the other side, they discovered a large natural pool filled with sparkling clear water. Reaching down, Justin took a handful and tasted it. "It's cool water and salty. This isn't from rain; it must come up with the tide from deep under the island."

Standing on the side, they could see most of the bottom was free from rock and appeared to be smooth, clean sand. Toward the center, it became darker indicating a greater depth. "Let's swim," he said, kicking off his shoes.

"You first," Sandy laughed. "I'm still thinking about those sharks."

Sandy watched as Justin walked into the pool and then swam about thirty feet out into the middle. Grabbing a deep breath, he dove toward the bottom, disappearing in the darker water. She breathed a sigh of relief when he finally surfaced and swam to the shore near her. "The water got cooler the deeper I went, so it must be coming out of some underground well or cave that connects to the ocean. Couldn't see very much down there, but I'm sure there are no sharks."

Sandy waded out toward Justin, feeling the cool water on her sunbaked skin. Justin met her as she finally lost the feel of the sand under her feet and began to float in the salty seawater. Scooping her up in his arms, he held her close and kissed her. "I've wanted to do that for a while, " he said, as she held him tightly, "but didn't want to offend Linda and Fredrich."

Leaning back in Justin's arm, as he floated her around the lake, Sandy replied, "I had a short conversation with Fredrich in which he asked how you and I were getting along. I hedged my words carefully, not wanting to put you in jeopardy, but he assured me he really didn't care what we did as long as we were happy. From the way he said it, I'm sure he assumes we aren't playing cards when we're together."

"We could tell him we were playing strip poker, just not using a deck of cards," Justin said as he held Sandy with one arm and stroked her shoulder with the other. "Great thing with that game is nobody ever loses."

Sandy ran a hand through Justin's dark hair and looked into his eyes. "Pick a number between one and ten."

Looking at her quizzically, Justin said, "Eight."

"Nope, you lose." Sandy laughed. "The number was three. You owe me an article of clothing."

Justin laughed as he threw Sandy up in the air, letting her land in the water where she quickly sank. When she surfaced, he was standing, holding his swim
trunks in his hand. "This will be a very short game, " he said, "that's the last and only item I have."

"Hmmmm, "Sandy smiled as she came close to him and took his exposed manhood into her hands, "let's see what else you could play with. Pick a number between one and ten."

Feeling his erection grow, as Sandy continued to lightly stroke it, Justin said, "Three."

"Nice try, but the number was five. Now you have to give me something that I would like, because you seem to have nothing to wear. Reaching behind her back, she unhooked her bikini top, and held it in her hand along with his trunks. Justin moved toward her, but she held up her hand motioning him to wait. Turning, she walked out of the water, slid off her bikini bottom and then slowly walked back to where he was standing. "Okay, Mr. I-don't-have-any-clothes-to-bet, better do something to pay your debt before I call the authorities."

Justin reach out and grabbed her around her waistline, pulling her near him. Lifting her, he drew her breast into his mouth and began to play with her nipple. Her skin was cool and salty from the water, but the nipple was rock hard in his mouth. Sandy held his head, as he pulled deeper on her nipple until he released it and worked his way to the other side.

Suddenly, he put his hands under her ass and dropped his body underwater. Sandy felt him pull her legs around his shoulders, and then she screamed as he pushed back to the surface. Holding onto the back of his head, she felt his tongue slide into her vaginal lips, searching for a deeper entry. Drawing her closer, his tongue finally spread her flushed lips and penetrated deeply into her. His mouth opened wide, allowing him to slide his tongue over places that sent ripples of excitement through her body.

At last, he pulled back and slowly settled her into the water. Her legs slipped off his shoulders, and he guided them down to his hips. She felt his stiff cock rub against her ass and lips. Floating lightly on the water while Justin held her lower back, Sandy reached down, took his erection in her hand and rubbed it on her well-exposed pussy. Her lips opened as she slowly pushed him inside, feeling the heat of his cock go deep into her.

Justin pulled her up as she slid her arms around his neck, kissed him, and pushed harder on his dick, forcing it even deeper inside her. Drawing close, she felt the heat of his body on her breasts and the throbbing of his dick deep inside her. "Don't move," she moaned, as he held her. "I just want to feel you in me."

Placing her feet on his ass, she spread her legs a little wider, squeezed tighter on his body, and at last felt the touch of his hard dick in the very back of her vagina. Her clit pressed so firmly against him, the slow rocking of their bodies in the water began to excite her beyond control. Holding him, she pressed harder, felt her clit become so sensitive she couldn't stand it and then experienced an orgasm deep within. Gripping him tightly, she uttered a gasp and then a loud moan.

Justin felt her vagina tighten as she pulled him. Touching the back of her womb with the end of his dick, he sensed her vaginal walls contract tightly. With a loud moan, she grasped him and then exploded; her warm juices flowed from her pussy over his deeply implanted erection. She continued to hold him tightly with each contraction continuing to ebb and flow within her, until at last she relaxed in his arms.

Looking into his eyes, she kissed him deeply and then looked down to observe his firm dick still inside her.

"That's one of the more beautiful things in life," he said quietly, watching her stare at their coupling. "It's a place of oneness that's more than just sex; it's a beautiful part of being together with someone who's special."

Still watching, she lifted her body until he was almost out of her and then slowly lowered until he once again disappeared. "I don't think I ever viewed it like this. The water helps me stay up here and watch," she whispered, drawing back and then pressing him in one more time. Lifting her body higher, she pulled him out, drew back her legs and holding his shoulders, began to rub her ass up and down his hard cock. Justin reached between her legs and grabbed his erection, as she slid her ass up higher. Placing his dick on her anus, he pushed in until he felt her relax and finally take him up into her.

Sandy wrapped her legs around him and slowly pulled him in deeper. The feeling within her was one of deep comfort and sheer ecstasy. Lifting away from his body, she pushed him out until he was about to exit and then drew him in again. The water made the entrance easier as Sandy began to move a little faster.

She sensed him getting even harder as he penetrated her tight ass and knew he was close to exploding.

Looking at her and feeling her tautness all around his cock, he reached down and pressed her firmly as her ass engulfed his hardness. She began to move faster and he knew it was almost time to pull out.

"Don't come out. Cum in me," she panted as she once again pulled and pushed harder and faster. Grasping him tightly, she felt the release start deep within her. Pushing hard on him, she felt his hot semen fill her. Grasping his neck tightly with one arm, she slid her other hand off of his neck and plunged between her legs into her vagina, joining him in her own orgasmic release.

Holding each other close, they allowed the cool waters of the pool to refresh their bodies until he finally pulled out and swept her up in his arms. Still breathing deeply, she placed her head on his shoulder, grasping his neck, as he walked to the edge of the water. Gently lowering her spent body to the sand on the shore, he stretched out next to her as she settled into his arms.

"You play a great game of strip poker," she said softly as she stroked his chest. "I really love what you do to my body. I'm amazed at the things we've done together in such a short time. I know you won't believe it, but I'm not always this aggressive."

"I believe you," he said, looking down on her beautiful naked flesh. "It may be the vacation away, the beauty of *Eclipse*, the need to just be crazy, who knows. I'm just happy we've been with each other. You're a beautiful woman, not only sexually, but in ways that make me feel whole. "

"One thing you missed in that thought," she said as she sat up on one arm and looked at him. "Maybe it's you who is bringing out this new me. I feel so relaxed and safe with you, and I don't know anything about you."

He laughed. "Maybe that's why you feel so safe, you don't know me. If you did you might feel differently."

Sitting up, Sandy looked at him. "Fredrich said you didn't have a criminal record but didn't tell me anything else. He just said sometimes it is better to just accept what people tell you and not dig deeper. I guess I should do that but something about you just doesn't fit."

Justin became a little concerned about the direction of the conversation but didn't want to just shut Sandy off without giving her something. "What doesn't fit?"

"You tell me you're just drifting from job to job and don't have any plans or roots, but you're obviously well educated with an intelligent perspective on a lot of different topics. You're a very attractive man who is a fantastic lover, yet you appear to be single without any companion or lover. Those things just don't fit, but Justin, believe me, if you don't want to disclose, I'll keep my thoughts to myself and just enjoy what we have right now."

Justin watched Sandy, as she went over her concerns, knowing that her declaration about not probing into his life was something she really meant, but not something she wanted to happen. She'd given him so much in such a short period, bringing a new inspiration to his rather bleak life. He had to give her something.

"I'm not all that mysterious," he said as brushed some sand off her shoulder and once again admired the beauty of this woman. "I've been married and it didn't work, so I've been hesitant to go at it again. We never had children and all my close family members are dead. My mom died when I was eight, leaving me with a difficult and unloving father. When I was old enough, I did my own thing, which was trying to do the opposite of everything the old man wanted me to do.

The last years have been difficult, trying to find myself, keeping other people happy, and not really succeeding at any of it. I finally got tired of a crap life and hit the road. I've bounced around until I met you. And now you know my story."

Sandy looked at Justin, realizing he carried a lot of hurt inside but didn't really want to expose it. She was positive what he shared wasn't easy for him. Nevertheless, she was also sure what he just told her was only a part of his life. He'd opened up, and now she needed to let him feel safe again. Reaching over, she gave him a kiss and said softly, "Thank you Justin, I know that type of thing wasn't easy for you, but I appreciate your sharing. I won't pry anymore, but I want you to know you are very habit forming, so I may at least have to have a phone number when our little adventure is over."

Jumping to her feet, she held out her hand. "Come on, let's get our gear back on and go look at the fish in the reefs. This has been a fantastic day, and I do appreciate you being in my life. "

As they picked up their suits and headed back to the beach, Justin thought about her request for a phone number when this was over. Part of him didn't want to lose Sandy, but another part wanted to lose Justin in the world that wouldn't find him. He was going to have to make a choice in a few days, but given his desire to drop out of life, he was afraid it would be painful for both of them.

Chapter 11

Spotting the raft heading back to their beach area, Sandy and Justin packed up the gear and waited for it to come ashore. Noticing that Linda was alone, they both wondered if everything was okay.

"We have a problem back in Palm Beach," she hollered to them as she drove the raft up on the sand. "Some transactions we thought were finished came unraveled and need our personal attention. I'm really sorry to do this, but we're going to have to head back early."

Sandy got in the raft, as Justin loaded the equipment and pushed them off the beach. She said, "I have no problem heading back. I'm just grateful for the time out here on *Eclipse*. I hope it isn't anything serious back in Palm Beach."

"We told you about the sale of the three yachts," Linda said as she turned the raft and headed back to *Eclipse*. "We thought it was a done deal, but apparently the bank for the buyer decided not to back the deal, and it all fell through."

"What boats are you selling off?" Justin asked.

"The two Cal sailboats and the 47 foot Silverton," Linda replied, "They're mostly paid for and will generate enough to take the debt down on the *Eclipse*."

Justin thought about this for a minute. "Won't that cut into your income-producing charters? I imagine you have a lot of people who can afford a trip on those who can't afford *Eclipse*."

"If we can increase the charters on *Eclipse* and lower our debt, we'll be in a better position. Unfortunately, this bank suddenly has cold feet, so Freddy is trying to see what he can come up with to salvage the deal."

They arrived back at *Eclipse* and secured the raft on deck. Linda asked Justin to check with Fredrich to see what he needed in order to get underway, and he headed up to the bridge. Sandy helped Linda stow the gear in its proper place and then followed her into the office space. The air conditioning was on providing a refreshingly cool break from the hot Florida sun.

"I think I need a drink," Linda said as she headed to the bar. "Want to join me?"

Sandy agreed, and they settled on the couch in the office, sipping on a vodka and fresh-squeezed orange juice. "Are you worried about this set back?" she asked Linda.

"Not worried, just concerned that it threw off the plans we thought were already implemented. The three boats are a drain on our maintenance, and we haven't booked charters on them thinking they'd be gone. Now they sit empty and we still have a big mortgage on *Eclipse*. Damn banks! Our buyer has great credit and the ability to pay the loan, but the bank is worried about the economy and isn't sure it wants to back an expansion of our buyer's charter business."

She took a sip of her drink and then turned to Sandy. "So, woman to woman, are you and Justin having fun? It's none of my business, but I really sense a connection between you two."

Sandy laughed. "Woman to woman, I've acted in ways that startle me in the last two days. I'm not a prude, but I find myself saying and doing things that I only fantasized about when I was in my own private room. I swear you put something in *Eclipse's* water that makes me a sex addict."

Linda laughed and almost spilled her drink. "No, honey, nothing in the water, but *Eclipse* does have a seductive flair about her. We've had some wild things take place here, and we've only had her a couple years. The sailboats used to be the places for wild sex, but this ship brings out the fantasy in everybody."

"I'm glad to hear that," Sandy said with a sigh of relief. "I thought I was becoming a sex addict in my old age."

"Hey there are a lot of addictions we could fall into," Linda said with a laugh, "but I think that one would be the most fun."

Sandy lifted her glass in a toast. "Linda, I will definitely drink to that."

Justin and Fredrich navigated through the reefs and then hit open water. Adjusting the autopilot, Fredrich turned to Justin. "I'm sorry to have to head back, but I can't get anybody to make sense over the phone, so I guess one-on-one is the only answer. When we get back, you stay on board if you want, we aren't going anyplace for a week.

Sandy will be here for another three days, so you can keep her company if you'd like."

"Not to pry," Justin said, "but what happened to your buyer? Didn't the bank secure the loan with him before he signed?"

"He had an agreement for the loan, but then the bank decided they didn't want to back a charter expansion in a bad economy. The buyer has been in business for twenty years and runs a very profitable company. He was going to replace some older equipment with the boats he bought from us. He already has charters to cover the season, so it just doesn't make sense."

Justin wrote something on a notepad and handed it to Fredrich. "When you get back to the dock, call this man at that number. It's in France, but the price of the call will be worth it. If he checks your buyer's figures and finds they are what you say, then this man will take the

124

loan. I'll drop an email to him to let him know you're calling. He owes me a lot of favors."

Fredrich held the note in his fingers like it was gold. "No shit!?"

Justin laughed. "No shit. Banks can be real asses to deal with, so I use private investors for large deals. I figure the three yachts you're selling will bring in about a million, which is change to these guys. It might be worth it to see if my friend wants to hold the mortgage on *Eclipse*. He'll give you a good rate and flexible terms, because I'll tell him to."

Fredrich looked at Justin for a while and then said quietly, "No shit?"

Justin clapped his hand on Fredrich's shoulder. "No shit. You have no idea how much this cruise has helped me. It's the least I can do. I know you have to tell Linda what the deal is and who I am, but ask her to keep it to herself. I still need to be anonymous for now. But if I ever decide to be me again, I may charter *Eclipse* out for a long time."

"Then I hope you become you real soon." Fredrich laughed. "How you doing with Sandy? Does she know who you are?"

Justin looked out over the ocean and sighed. "In some ways she knows me better than anyone ever did, but she doesn't know my identity. I'm just not ready to head back into life, yet I don't want to lose the friendship we've developed. Guess I'll have to face that soon."

"Well, stick around as long as you want," Fredrich said. "Hell, you can live with us if you want. You just saved my neck."

"Thanks for the offer, Fredrich. It is tempting, but I'm just not settled within myself yet and think I have to keep moving. I'll be back after I figure out what I'm looking for in my life; I guarantee that."

"I've got one drink with alcohol and one without," Linda said as she and Sandy entered the bridge. "Who's driving?"

Fredrich laughed as he gave her a hug. "Right now *Eclipse* is driving herself, but I'll be on duty when we come to dock. Give the alcohol to Justin. He's off duty for the rest of the day. I need to talk to you for a few minutes, so why don't we go to the office? Justin and Sandy, you have the run of the ship, so go enjoy your time at sea."

Putting his arm around Linda, Fredrich turned to Justin and smiled. "I'm really happy you came along. Wish I could talk you into a full-time position, but I understand you have to be you."

As they exited toward the office, Sandy sat in the captain's chair and looked out at the perfectly calm waters. "They are a great couple. I hope everything works out for them."

Sitting in the chair opposite her, Justin took a sip of his drink as he stretched out his legs. "They run a good business, which is important to financial institutions. I know they'll work through this without any problems. How are you doing with their book?"

Still looking out over the water, Sandy said, "I've thought a lot about what I want to do, but I've been a little distracted by this sailor I met on the ship."

"I know, I'm sorry I haven't let you spend more time at your work. Nevertheless, if I had to do it all over again, I'd do the same thing."

Sandy turned to face him. "You seem to be in such a peaceful place on the ship, and it sound like Fredrich would jump at the opportunity to have you stay, why do you have to keep moving?"

Justin hesitated as he considered his words. "I'm forty-five years old, Sandy; done a lot of good things and a lot of not so good things. A few weeks ago, I decided I hated life and wanted to drop out. Didn't hate it enough to kill myself, just enough to drop out. For a lot of reasons, I've never trusted people enough to let my guard down, and that left me with a very empty life."

He turned to face her. "From the minute I saw the flyer about the *Eclipse* I seem to have been on some autopilot that I don't understand. I'm not a deeply spiritual man, but I think I was supposed to be here for a reason. Some of that reason I understand, but most of it just seems difficult to grasp. You're part of my 'difficult to grasp' portion."

"Me?" she said, looking at him intently, "What did I do?"

"You let me enjoy life like I haven't in years. Not just our sexual exploits, which are the most fun I have ever had, but simply watching you and feeling your confidence. When I first met you down on the main deck, you spun me, and I still don't know why. Since then, I look forward to simply being with you and believe me, I've never looked forward to being with anyone for very long."

Neither spoke for a few minutes as they simply sat and looked at each other. "Fuck," Sandy finally said.

"Is that a request or a complaint?" Justin asked with a smile.

Sandy reached into her glass, grasped an ice cube and threw it at him. "Neither. It was a statement about my life."

Ducking the frozen missile, Justin laughed. "I'm sorry, I couldn't resist. What did you mean? You seem to guide your life the way you want it to go. Why is it so bad?"

"I see a complication on the horizon, and it seems to have disappointment written all over it. It may be hard for you to believe, but I've been more relaxed and filled with happiness in the last two days than I have been since I was much younger. I've shared my life and my body with a man who

I enjoy more than anything, yet I know I have to detach from him because he's a drifter who doesn't want anything permanent.

"Then he tells me that I'm special to him, and I feel a every solid, rational defense mechanism start to crash around me. I know where this is headed Justin; a memory never to be forgotten but just a memory."

"Sandy, the last thing I ever want to do is hurt you."

"I know and you have to believe me when I tell you I don't hold you responsible for how I feel or even for what I know will be pain when I leave you. I'm old enough to know that fantasy is just that: fantasy. I don't want you to change or to feel you have to protect me from myself. All I want is to live in the moment until the fantasy is over."

Standing, she went to his side and kissed him. "We have something special that is wonderful. I refuse to lose it to

131

complications. Let's just go lay in the sun and enjoy the moment."

Justin took her hand and pulled her close. "One last thought. I promise you, when I settle my inner conflicts, I will find you."

Sandy kissed him and then ran her fingers through his hair. "Okay, sailor, I'll wait for your call. Come on, let's go seize the day."

Chapter 12

They secured *Eclipse* to the dock as
the last rays of sun were turning the sky
into a pallet of colors. Fredrich and
Linda went to the company office after
providing some directions to a local
restaurant they both enjoyed. They
promised Sandy they would catch up with
her on *Eclipse* in the morning so they
could work on the book. Before they left,
Linda wrapped her arms around Justin and
gave him a big hug. She turned quickly
and left the boat but not before Sandy
caught the tears in her eyes.

"What was that all about?" she asked
Justin as they headed to their suites.

"I have no idea," he said. "I don't
know about you, but I'm starved. Let me

change and then I'll take you to that special restaurant they recommended."

"You got a deal, sailor." She laughed but remained somewhat confused by Linda's reaction to Justin.

Returning to her suite, she shed her bikini and wandered into the shower. Three days ago she'd been sitting in the winter of New York, periodically masturbating to porn, going about her life and not really thinking about the future. In the last forty-eight hours, she found herself transformed into a Cinderella who arrived at the castle and found a Prince Charming who swept her off her feet. In this floating castle she lived in luxury, had sex beyond her wildest imagination, enjoyed the company of her prince as if in a dream, and found a new energy to her life that she had forgotten.

"Fuck."

"I have to stop saying that," she said to the water that ran over her flesh. Nevertheless, it did reflect the unrest that continued to grow within her. "Just enjoy what you have and stop being such a baby!" Standing in the water, she felt the pangs of unrest release within as the tears started to roll down her cheeks. Slowly they grew into sobs as she lowered her body to the shower floor and allowed the agony to unfurl from within. Over the last few years, she lived behind her wall of invincibility pretending that she was happy being independent and alone; now it was all crashing around her, and she couldn't stop it. Justin would leave, and in spite of his promise to find her, she knew he never would. Her choice was to either live in a place of pain, or return to the hiding place behind the wall. It wasn't really a choice; it was a necessary retreat if she was going to survive. Standing again, she washed the tears from her face and turned off the shower. "I'll go back to my wall tomorrow," she said softly. "But for now I will just allow myself to feel loved."

Sandy had finished her makeup and just slipped on a light dress when she heard Justin knock on her door. Opening it, she was surprised to find him standing with a large bouquet of the most beautiful white roses she had ever seen.

"Where did you find these?" she exclaimed as he handed them to her.

"Found a florist nearby who would deliver. In France we would say they are a blanche fleur, or white rose. I thought they fit you perfectly."

"Blanche Fleur, was Percival's mystical love who captured his heart and gave him strength for his conquests," Sandy said as she put the roses in a vase nearby.

"You know the story," Justin said smiling.

"Thank you, Justin, they are beautiful."

He came behind her and kissed her neck. "You, my Blanche Fleur, are more beautiful than the flowers. You need to live in sunshine where you can have a healthy tan year round."

She turned and kissed him, allowing herself to feel the love without hesitation. In her mind, she remembered the fable of Blanche Fleur ended with both she and Percival dying, but she chose to let that thought slip by without comment.

Leaving *Eclipse* behind, they entered Justin's car and followed the Allens' directions to a beautiful restaurant nestled on the shore of the intercostal. The palm trees and Spanish moss provided a tropical setting that played host to an almost full moon in the evening sky. Fredrich had apparently notified the owner they were coming, which allowed them to have a private booth on a small pier. Sitting in the warm evening breeze, Sandy looked at the moon and smiled.

"What's so funny?" Justin asked, reaching over and taking her hand.

"I have this Cinderella fantasy going on in my head, and this table fits into it perfectly. My prince has provided a perfect environment for Cinderella so she may bask in all the joy her life is offering. He even gave her white roses and called her Blanche Fleur; a touch that only a prince could provide."

"You deserve the best, my Blanche Fleur; you are truly the princess of the domain." He kissed her fingers as the waiter came to take their order, missing the small tear that Sandy quickly wiped from her eye.

From the first glass of wine to the final aperitif, dinner was fantastic. They easily shared thoughts and conversation as if old friends, while they watched the moon move across the water, casting its white trail on the rolling inter-coastal waves. Driving back to the ship, they both fell into a quiet place that wasn't uncomfortable. It was a calm place filled with its own energy. As he helped her out of the car, she paused and looked at him. "My prince, can I have one more request to this enchanted evening?"

"Your wish is my command," he said, brushing a lock of hair from her face.

"Make love to me tonight," she whispered. "Make long, slow love to me."

Kissing her, he took her hand and without a word, headed to *Eclipse*.

In her suite, Justin fixed a drink, as Sandy played with the Satellite radio until she found something that fit her mood. As she sat on the couch, he handed her a drink and then sat across from her. "Can the prince also have a wish granted on this wonderful night?" he asked.

Smiling, she said, "Your wish is my command."

I want to look at you sitting there without your dress. I want to look at you and enjoy the beauty of who you are while we talk."

Sandy set her drink on the table, pulled the dress over her head, revealing that once again, she was naked underneath. Picking up her glass, she said, "To the *Eclipse*, and all she has given us."

"You look like a painting as you sit in the soft light, stretched out on the couch. You're a very beautiful woman, Sandy. I know I keep saying that, but I really mean it."

Laughing, Sandy said, "Oh please don't tell me that, Oh stop, stop."

Stretching out she ran her hand down her body. " A few years ago you wouldn't have said that so easily. I was about thirty to forty pounds heavier and a rather disheveled woman."

"You would have still been beautiful; just more of you to admire."

"Oh listen to mister smooth over there." She laughed. "No, my marriage destroyed me and I really let myself go. My ex couldn't keep his dick in his pants, so I assumed it was my fault. Rather than trying to improve, I just gave up. It is amazing how a divorce from a bastard can improve your disposition."

Justin moved and sat next to her. "You're a strong woman to be able to recover from that type of pain. I think that's part of my problem; I keep all the crap within me and don't let it go. I allow it to color my thoughts."

Sandy turned and put her head on his lap as she stretched out on her back. "Crap from your marriage?" she asked.

"No, crap from my father. After my mother died, he was determined to make me a man like him. He was a cold, detached, miserable son of a bitch who I gradually came to hate. I rebelled against him all my life until he died, and then I became like him."

Looking up at him she exclaimed, "You may be a lot of things, but you're not a cold, detached, miserable son of a bitch, Justin."

He ran his hand over her shoulder and lightly stroked each breast. "Maybe I'm not to you, but I think this is the first time I ever admitted I'd become what he wanted. Perhaps that epiphany is what I've been looking for in my search. I began to hate myself as much as I hated him, yet in many ways, he was the only role model I had to work with from my past."

Sandy sat up and put her arms around him. "Who you have been the last few days is who you really are. Believe in that. It's the way I see you, and I always will."

Justin pulled her close and held her for a long time, neither speaking a word until he slid his arm under her and walked her to the bed. He gently placed her down, quietly undressed and then lay beside her.

"Thank you for listening to me, Sandy. I never said those things to anyone before. I think my Blanche Fleur, is a healer in disguise."

Pulling close to him she whispered, "I don't have enough clothes on to disguise much."

"I think that is part of my healing,."

Their lips met as they settled into an intimate embrace allowing both their bodies and souls to be one. "Go inside me and hold me," she whispered as she moved on top of him. "I just want to be one with you."

Reaching down she took his erection and slowly placed it inside her already moist lips. Pushing down she felt the ecstasy of their joining.

"Oh god, Justin, I so love being with you," she moaned as she pushed him deeper into her body.

Holding her, he ran his hands down her back, gently squeezing, as she enveloped him. They kissed passionately as they enjoyed the sensation of loving their sexuality without having to move.

He finally rolled her on her back as he remained deep inside her pulsating vagina. "I love looking at you. That first night, when you fell asleep, I stayed for a long time and just looked at you." Reaching down, he kissed her, and then moved his lips to her breasts, softly touching her erect nipples with his tongue. Feeling her tighten deep inside, he slowly slid out and then gently reentered her, watching her face express the pleasure she was feeling.

"Take me up the mountain, and then let me fly," she whispered with shallow breath.

Justin started moving slowly out of her and then back in deeply until his body pressed down on her now sensitive clit, sending ripples of pleasure throughout her. Pulling her legs up, she forced her eyes open and watched his face, as he continued to increase the tempo of their passion. As the pressure within her increased, she let herself go and felt the ripple of orgasm turn into waves that finally sent her crashing into oblivion. Grasping him tightly, she felt him continue to touch places within her that released electricity. "Take me from behind, please," she panted.

Turning her on her stomach, he pressed her down until she lay flat. She then experienced his hardness slide between her legs as it moved between her folds and pressed on her clit. Not entering her, he continued to move up and down, exciting her until she once again lost herself in a sea of orgasm.

At last, he pulled up and lifted her ass in the air while she pressed her breasts onto the bed. Glancing over, she saw him open a condom, and then she felt him slide deep into her; deeper than she had ever experienced. Holding her ass tightly, he began to thrust deeply, rapidly filling her with his dick until she thought she would scream. Grabbing the bed covers, she gripped them tightly, feeling like she was going to explode into a thousand pieces. Each time he entered her she felt a sense of being totally possessed by him, and she wanted him to take all of her.

Suddenly, she could no longer catch a breath, as her body was overcome by a convulsion that literally touched every muscle. She knew she was screaming into the pillow but couldn't stop until she felt him release within her. At that moment, she tumbled off the mountain and fell down into the darkness below.

Aware she was trying to breathe into the pillow as she continued to grip the bed covers tightly, Sandy uncurled her fingers, turned her head and finally took a deep breath. Justin moved out of her and rolled onto his back laying quietly, breathing deeply.

"Holy shit," she murmured as she slowly moved to her back, "I think I just died, and if so, I love dying."

Justin pulled her limp body close and she snuggled into him. "I don't think I ever made love to a woman before," he said quietly. "Maybe I never loved before."

"Me either," she said groggily. But before she could say more, sleep overwhelmed her spent body.

Chapter 13

Sandy felt the motion as the boat suddenly lurched to the side. Jumping out of bed, she realized the deck under her feet was leaning sharply; a sign something was radically wrong. Moving toward the door, she glanced out the window only to see the blue water of the ocean starting to move up and close out the sun. Opening the door, she was greeted with a rush of cold water that flashed into her cabin, knocking her to her knees. Struggling toward the door, she navigated the hall until she reached the stair to the bridge.

Quickly ascending the staircase, she dashed into the bridge to find Justin sitting in the captain's chair sipping a cup of coffee. Slowly he turned to her and smiled as he took another sip. "You are quite naked, Sandy; not really an appropriate display for a sinking ship."

"Justin, what's going on with the ship? Why are we sinking?"

Smiling, he stood and walked up to her. "I decided I was finished with the ship, and it was time to sink it. It is my decision, and I think it is a good one. However, it might be a good idea for you to get off soon, as she is about to go down for the last time. Personally, I like you naked, but you probably will want to be dressed once you get to the office."

The ship lurched sharply, and she saw water begin to flood the bridge. "What about you? Are you coming?"

Justin laughed. "That's my concern, not yours. Goodbye, Sandy, get dressed soon."

The water began to flood over her, as she frantically headed toward the deck door. She was now underwater and couldn't

seem to move out of the bridge.
Frantically she turned toward Justin, but
he was no longer there. The water was
pulling her into the ship, as *Eclipse*
headed toward the bottom of the sea.

Sitting up with a jolt, Sandy gasped
in a deep breath as she threw back the
covers. Glancing around the suite, she
realized she'd been dreaming and slowly
laid back, trying to catch her breath.
Feeling her heart start to calm, she took
a deep breath, and sat up in the bed. The
sun was just above the horizon, as she
looked at the clock, which reported six
thirty.

Looking around, she saw she was
alone in the room. Justin had apparently
left sometime during the night. Now more
relaxed, she remembered their fantastic
night together, as well as the
overwhelming sex they'd shared. Looking
over at her nightstand, she spied a white
rose on top of what appeared to be a
handwritten note. Fear gripped her heart.

Her dream suddenly became a reality, as she knew what was in the note. Justin was gone, and she was left alone on the sinking dreams of all they shared. She stared at the note, feeling her stomach turn into a knot that caused her to sense she was about to vomit. "Oh, Justin, why?"

There came no reply; only the empty room with a white rose and an unread note. Breathing deeply, she pulled up her knees and rolled toward her side. "I can handle this," she said aloud as she hugged her knees close. Part of her wished he'd at least said goodbye, but she knew that when he left, she would only have the comfort of the good memories to help her through the pain.

Lowering her knees, she felt her stomach relax as she pulled the covers over her body. They'd shared a few fantastic days together, but she knew from the beginning he was someone who would leave her when the party was over.

It would have been nice if the party had
lasted longer, but what was the
difference? It would always end the same
way no matter what the day or time.

He'd shared so much of himself last
night and yet had shared so little. What
had his father done to him that made him
so bitter? Obviously, losing a mother at
such a young age would impact any child,
but the hatred of his father seemed to be
grounded in something much deeper. Part
of her wanted to help him come into a
place of healing, but she knew that
ultimately it was his journey and not
hers.

She picked up the white rose and
held it to her nose, smelling the sweet
fragrance. *Blanche Fleur*. How her heart
had melted when he called her that name,
even if it was from a myth that ended
badly. Maybe that's why he chose that
name; he knew the end of this story.

No, Justin wasn't a person who
intended to harm; he was a gentle,

loving, lost man, who transformed her life beyond her wildest expectation. Placing the rose on her lips, she felt the sorrow rise within her, forcing her to replace it with the memories of their last few days; memories that brought smiles to the broken pieces within her.

She picked up the note and opened it, discovering a handwritten message that covered the page. The first words read, *"Dearest Sandy,"* Tears filled her eyes as she read the words. How she wanted to hear him say those words, but only the memory of his voice could now fill the void.

"I sit here in the chair next to your bed, watching as you sleep ever so deeply. This is the second time I have intruded on your private moments, and I so appreciate the times that I can't even try to feel guilty about stealing them. We have spent so few hours together, yet they seem to have been a lifetime of emotions. I taught myself to be detached,

yet from my first sighting of you I was
hopelessly caught in your trap. I didn't
fight to get out. I simply decided to see
what you would do with your ensnared
prey.

To my surprise, you brought a
healing to my broken soul, and I found
your snare was not a trap but a release.
I told you last night that I'd never made
love to a woman, and that statement is so
true I found it hard to believe I hadn't
seen it before. I have had sex, but I've
never made love. As I have thought about
it these last few hours, I realized why.
I have never allowed myself to love. So
my journey to disappear has now
confronted me with two truths: I have
become like my father, and I have never
loved. That is not bad for a two-week
adventure into discovering truth.

So what now? First, I have not been
honest with you. I have been married
twice. Once at nineteen, which lasted six
months, and once at thirty--a vivid

mistake that took four years to unravel. So I am not a person with a great track record.

Second, I am not just a wandering vagrant who works on tramp steamers. I have some financial stability, which I will explain another time.

Third, I have decided to stop running from my life and try to be the person you tell me I am. Maybe with help, I can accomplish this.

Fourth, I am accomplished at one thing, which I take deep pride in sharing with others: I make a wonderful cup of coffee.

So, dearest Sandy, if you're up for whatever the future holds, I would like to share that adventure with you. If you would like to join me in this journey, come up to the bridge for a cup of coffee. I think I have never loved before, but I believe I have found a place to begin. I hope you feel the same.

Love,

Justin

Sandy dropped the note and stared out the window. Picking it up again, she read the last few paragraphs, threw back the covers, ran to the door and headed toward the stairs. Halfway up, she realized she was stark naked and turned to go back. Then she stopped, and with tears in her eyes, and a smile on her face, she bounded up the stairs toward a wonderful smell of fresh coffee.

"Carpe Diem," she whispered as she ran onto the bridge and into Justin's waiting arms.

The End

If you enjoyed this story, Join "J" on her website www.J-Erotica.com as she takes you on an adventure into love, romance, and sexual pleasure. Find samples of her other books and share in her new book:

At the Rooftop

Spending a weekend at a clothing optional lifestyle resort can only lead to one thing: pleasure. Join in the fun as the term 'being free' takes on a whole new meaning. For your pleasure, here is chapter one.

Chapter 1

The drop of perspiration ran down the back of Charlotte's neck, then dove between her shoulder blades. She felt it but chose not to move. The heat of the sun would dry the moisture, and it was just too hot to turn over. Besides, the sun was penetrating deep into her flesh, and she knew she would pay the price for her lazy moment; especially on her naked ass that was not used to this much exposure.

For that matter, this weekend had all the indications that it would produce a limelight to areas in her life that weren't accustomed to this much exposure. Not that she had regrets or felt victimized; she'd come here willingly with her eyes wide open. It was simply different when you're living in the reality instead of living in the fantasy.

Letting out a long sigh, she rolled into a sitting position and felt the small pool of perspiration roll down her spine and finally find a resting place in the crack of her ass. Feeling the gentle breeze from the ocean, she stretched her body and once again regarded her new surroundings. Sitting six floors above the hot Florida pavement, the Rooftop Resort Hotel was an inviting and relaxing place to just drop out. It was an older hotel that had been refurbished to fit the new owner's design. While rather plain and unobtrusive from the exterior, the interior had an atmosphere of a party. From the vivid nudes on the lobby walls to the sign on the entrance wall stating, "Nude swimming is encouraged," Rooftop Resort Hotel was pure fun.

She was now on the rooftop itself in an area filled with chaise lounges that were beginning to be occupied in the early afternoon sun. The bar in the corner provided both shade and refreshment, but the huge pool was the main attraction on the rooftop. Skinny dipping on the roof of a building and being joined by other guests in the hotel was definitely a different experience. These guests all shared one thing in common on this hot afternoon: they were all either naked or as close to it as possible. Charlotte perused her own body and realized the places not generally exposed to the sun were showing a bit of redness.

"You okay, baby?" the voice next to her asked. Charlotte reached out and stroked the naked back of her friend and smiled. "I'm okay, but we're both getting a little red. I'm going in the water for a minute and then heading to the bar. I think you should consider doing the same, Joey."

Joey pulled her sunglasses down and leaned up on her elbows. "I think you're right. I need a bathroom run, and then I'll join you in the pool." Pulling a baseball cap on her head, Joey rose from the lounge and stretched. "What time is it anyway?"

Charlotte looked at her watch, "Three forty-five. That's two hours out here; it's shade time."

Standing, Joey looked around the pool in order to check out the local inhabitants. She ran her hand over her breast and down her belly. "Okay, Char, be right back."

Charlotte observed Joey leave and once again admired the muscular back which reflected months of working out in the gym. Joey wasn't as tall as Charlotte's five foot seven frame, but her personality made her seem larger than life. With dark hair and beautiful green eyes, Joey was sexy, beautiful, and fun. Her taught body remained a vivid testimony to all the hard work they had put forth getting into shape. Meeting during those grueling workouts at the gym, they'd slowly developed a strong, trusting friendship. The sexual part of their relationship developed as a gradual evolution, which had no actual beginning, just a series of moments that seemed to fit together. Charlotte smiled as she finally walked to the edge of the pool. One thing about being with Joey, you never knew where things would lead. Thus, here they were, naked in Florida, not really knowing why but definitely believing life was good. With that thought, she dove into the pool and felt the heat of her flesh cry out in relief.

Standing in the water, she did a few stretches to get the blood flowing in her muscles. They'd promised each other to exercise while on vacation, but as of day two, they hadn't even tried. She felt someone's hands go around her and squeeze her breasts. Recognizing both the finger rings and the breasts pressing into her back, Charlotte leaned back into Joey's arms.

"You feel good, Char," Joey said as she wrapped her arms around Charlotte and held her. "Warm and slippery; my kind of woman."

Resting in Joey's embrace, Charlotte lifted her feet off the bottom. "I could get used to living like this," she murmured, as Joey slowly drifted her around the pool. They'd made a last minute decision to flee the northern winter months and head to Florida. Joey found an advertisement on the Internet for the Rooftop Resort Hotel in Hollywood, Florida, a place that catered to lifestyle living, which included a nude pool on the roof and clothing optional throughout the hotel. The hotel had about fifty rooms and provided a very private, yet casual, atmosphere. Obviously catering to people in the freedom of sexual lifestyle, Rooftop provided an open and tranquil atmosphere to be and do whatever you wanted at the moment. It was close to the beach, but the lack of clothing could only take place within the hotel itself.

Charlotte had never been in a clothing-optional environment, and Joey convinced her it was time to break into new territory. She smiled as she thought back to the Charlotte she was a few years ago and knew she had come a long way. Married too young to the wrong person almost destroyed her emotionally. She finished law school and filed for divorce the same month. As much as she tried to convince herself it was all her husband's problem, Charlotte knew she was also at fault. She'd married because her rather religious family expected it. She wanted to simply live together for a while and then decide, but she finally succumbed to the pressure of her parents, and plunged into an abyss that almost sucked the life out of her. By twenty-four she was a divorced woman, thirty pounds overweight, and afraid to ever try relationships again.

Taking a job at a law firm in Manhattan, she left behind her broken life in Philadelphia with a determination to live a new beginning. After a year of getting settled in the new job and environment of Manhattan, she finally joined the gym, beginning the long trek back to a healthy body. Getting close to thirty, she now prided herself on her tight stomach and firm ass. Joey

convinced her to lighten her hair to pure
blonde, a move she was now happy to have
made. Joey voiced her opinion that
Charlotte's blue eyes deserved blonde
hair, and Charlotte said okay. She was
afraid that the blonde hair might give
her a look of a brainless individual, but
Joey also told her if anyone felt that
way, Charlotte really didn't need to be
his or her friend.

   Meeting Joey began a physical
transformation and an emotional
metamorphosis. She and Joey loved each
other deeply and intimately, but both
knew they also desired to share their
lives with men. Joey had never been
married. Her goal was to stay single
until she hit thirty and then start to
find a relationship with a man that could
turn permanent. Meanwhile, Joey had a
large group of close friends and dated
quite easily. While Charlotte was still
very hesitant about long-term commitment,
she'd grown comfortable with dating

around until she might discover someone who would change her mind. Being with Joey was a safe place to explore her vastly-improved outlook on life. Having just celebrated their twenty-eighth birthdays, neither of them was rushing into anything.

"I need a drink," Joey proclaimed, releasing Charlotte and swimming to the poolside. "I'll get a couple towels and meet you at the bar. Get me a Corona Lite."

Charlotte pushed up on the pool ledge and headed toward the bar in the corner. She noticed a few more people had arrived and felt a little self-conscious as she walked to the bar totally naked. Most of the other people were either undressed or heading in that direction, but it was still a rather new experience for Charlotte, and one that would take a little more getting used to. They arrived late Thursday afternoon and found the hotel was sparsely occupied. Apparently most people came Friday through Monday in order to enjoy the long weekend in the sun.

Manny, the bartender, was busily loading up ice and glasses when Charlotte arrived.

"Hey, Charlotte, you through cooking in the sun?"

"Yeah, Manny, I think I'm burning my butt and need to get into the shade. Can you fix me two Corona Lites with lime and a bottle of water?

He smiled and set a bottle of water on the bar. "You guys find something to do last night?"

Charlotte opened the water. "We went across the street for dinner and then just sat around the pool and watched the stars." Actually, she and Joey had partaken of a few too many margaritas at the bar and ended up having a great sexual romp on one of the canopy beds on the rooftop. She was sure there were others somewhere near them, but the passion and the rum worked together to provide a façade of privacy, which they both believed to be real.

Setting the two beers on the bar he said, "Well tonight will provide more people 'cause Friday and Saturday is party time, so get your rest while you can. Got a great DJ Saturday night, so should be a good weekend."

Joey walked up and threw the towels on the bar stools. "Whew, it feels a lot better in the shade! Look, I got sunburn on my tits, and I covered them with lotion!"

"See, that's what you get for making them so big." Charlotte laughed. Joey had implants about six months ago resulting in breasts that were about two sizes larger. While they were beautiful to look at, Charlotte decided she didn't like the feel as much and opted out of having it done. She was a nice 34c and happy with that.

What's going on tonight, Manny?"
Joey asked as she sat on the stool and
took a large gulp from her beer.

"Reservations show about thirty new
people coming tonight, so should be a
good party. We're going to order pizza
for everyone around six; that will give
everyone a chance to meet and greet. You
guys looking for others or are you just
here as a couple?"

"Manny, " Joey said with a grin, "We
are into each other and whatever trouble
we can find. This is a vacation, it is
eighty degrees, and we are naked. Honey,
life is good."

Charlotte laughed as she looked out
over the rooftop and watched the waves
roll in on the beach. Life is good, she
thought, very good.

To learn more about J and her sensual exploits, go to

www.J-erotica.com

www.ingramcontent.com/pod-product-compliance
Lightning Source LLC
Chambersburg PA
CBHW070924130626
46555CB00001B/277